ACCLAIM FOR COLLEEN COBLE

"Prepare to stay up all night with Colleen Coble. Coble's beautiful, emotional prose coupled with her keen sense of pacing, escalating danger, and very real characters place her firmly at the top of the suspense genre. I could not put this book down."

—ALLISON BRENNAN, *NEW YORK TIMES* BESTSELLING AUTHOR
OF *SHATTERED* ON *THE VIEW FROM RAINSHADOW BAY*

"Bestselling author Colleen Coble elevates her already considerable suspense chops ..."

—*PUBLISHERS WEEKLY* ON *BENEATH COPPER FALLS*

"I loved returning to Rock Harbor and you will too. *Beneath Copper Falls* is Colleen at her best!"

—DANI PETTREY, BESTSELLING AUTHOR OF THE ALASKAN
COURAGE AND CHESAPEAKE VALOR SERIES

"Return to Rock Harbor for Colleen Coble's best story to date. *Beneath Copper Falls* is a twisting, turning, thrill ride from page one that drops you head first into danger that will leave you breathless, sleep deprived, and eager for more! I couldn't turn the pages fast enough!"

—LYNETTE EASON, AWARD-WINNING, BESTSELLING
AUTHOR OF THE ELITE GUARDIANS SERIES

"The tension, both suspenseful and romantic, is gripping, reflecting Coble's prowess with the genre."

—*PUBLISHERS WEEKLY*, STARRED REVIEW FOR
TWILIGHT AT BLUEBERRY BARRENS

"Incredible storytelling and intricately drawn characters. You won't want to miss *Twilight at Blueberry Barrens*!"

—BRENDA NOVAK, *NEW YORK TIMES* AND
USA TODAY BESTSELLING AUTHOR

"Coble has a gift for making a setting come to life. After reading *Twilight at Blueberry Barrens*, I feel like I've lived in Maine all my life. This plot kept me guessing until the end, and her characters seem like my friends. I don't want to let them go!"

—TERRI BLACKSTOCK, *USA TODAY*
BESTSELLING AUTHOR OF *IF I RUN*

"I'm a long-time fan of Colleen Coble, and *Twilight at Blueberry Barrens* is the perfect example of why. Coble delivers riveting suspense, delicious romance, and carefully crafted characters, all with the deft hand of a veteran writer. If you love romantic suspense, pick this one up. You won't be disappointed!"

—DENISE HUNTER, AUTHOR OF *THE GOODBYE BRIDE*

"Colleen Coble, the queen of Christian romantic mysteries, is back with her best book yet. Filled with familiar characters, plot twists, and a confusion of antagonists, I couldn't keep the pages of this novel set in Maine turning fast enough. I reconnected with characters I love while taking a journey filled with murder, suspense, and the prospect of love. This truly is her best book to date, and perfect for readers who adore a page-turner laced with romance."

—CARA PUTMAN, AWARD-WINNING AUTHOR
OF *SHADOWED BY GRACE* AND *WHERE TREETOPS
GLISTEN*, ON *TWILIGHT AT BLUEBERRY BARRENS*

"Gripping! Colleen Coble has again written a page-turning romantic suspense with *Twilight at Blueberry Barrens*! Not only did she keep me up nights racing through the pages to see what would happen next, I genuinely cared for her characters. Colleen sets the bar high for romantic suspense!"

—CARRIE STUART PARKS, AUTHOR OF *A CRY FROM THE DUST* AND *WHEN DEATH DRAWS NEAR*

"Colleen Coble thrills readers again with her newest novel, an addictive suspense trenched in family, betrayal, and . . . murder."

—DIANN MILLS, AUTHOR OF *DEADLY ENCOUNTER*, ON *TWILIGHT AT BLUEBERRY BARRENS*

"Coble's latest, *Twilight at Blueberry Barrens*, is one of her best yet! With characters you want to know in person, a perfect setting, and a plot that had me holding my breath, laughing, and crying, this story will stay with the reader long after the book is closed. My highest recommendation."

—ROBIN CAROLL, BESTSELLING NOVELIST

"Colleen's *Twilight at Blueberry Barrens* is filled with a bevy of twists and surprises, a wonderful romance, and the warmth of family love. I couldn't have asked for more. This author has always been a five-star novelist, but I think it's time to up the ante with this book. It's on my keeping shelf!"

—HANNAH ALEXANDER, AUTHOR OF THE HALLOWED HALLS SERIES

"Second chances, old flames, and startling new revelations combine to form a story filled with faith, trial, forgiveness, and redemption. Crack the cover and step in, but beware—Mermaid Moon is harboring secrets that will keep you guessing."

—LISA WINGATE, *NEW YORK TIMES* BESTSELLING AUTHOR OF *BEFORE WE WERE YOURS*, ON *MERMAID MOON*

"I burned through *The Inn at Ocean's Edge* in one sitting. An intricate plot by a master storyteller. Colleen Coble has done it again with this gripping opening to a new series. I can't wait to spend more time at Sunset Cove."

—HEATHER BURCH, BESTSELLING AUTHOR OF *ONE LAVENDER RIBBON*

"Coble doesn't disappoint with her custom blend of suspense and romance."

—*PUBLISHERS WEEKLY* ON *THE INN AT OCEAN'S EDGE*

"Veteran author Coble has penned another winner. Filled with mystery and romance that are unpredictable until the last page, this novel will grip readers long past when they should put their books down. Recommended to readers of contemporary mysteries."

—*CBA RETAILERS + RESOURCES* REVIEW OF *THE INN AT OCEAN'S EDGE*

"Coble truly shines when she's penning a mystery, and this tale will really keep the reader guessing . . . Mystery lovers will definitely want to put this book on their purchase list."

—*RT BOOK REVIEWS* ON *THE INN AT OCEAN'S EDGE*

"Master storyteller Colleen Coble has done it again. *The Inn at Ocean's Edge* is an intricately woven, well-crafted story of romance, suspense, family secrets, and a decades-old mystery. Needless to say, it had me hooked from page one. I simply couldn't stop turning the pages. This one's going on my keeper shelf."

—LYNETTE EASON, AWARD-WINNING, BESTSELLING
AUTHOR OF THE HIDDEN IDENTITY SERIES

"Evocative and gripping, *The Inn at Ocean's Edge* will keep you flipping pages long into the night."

—DANI PETTREY, BESTSELLING AUTHOR OF
THE ALASKAN COURAGE SERIES

"Coble's atmospheric and suspenseful series launch should appeal to fans of Tracie Peterson and other authors of Christian romantic suspense."

—*LIBRARY JOURNAL* REVIEW OF *TIDEWATER INN*

"Romantically tense, but with just the right touch of danger, this cowboy love story is surprisingly clever—and pleasingly sweet."

—USAToday.com REVIEW OF *BLUE MOON PROMISE*

"[An] outstanding, completely engaging tale that will have you on the edge of your seat . . . A must-have for all fans of romantic suspense!"

—THEROMANCEREADERSCONNECTION.
COM REVIEW OF *ANATHEMA*

"Colleen Coble lays an intricate trail in *Without a Trace* and draws the reader on like a hound with a scent."

—*RT BOOK REVIEWS*, 4½ STARS

"Coble's historical series just keeps getting better with each entry."

—*LIBRARY JOURNAL* STARRED REVIEW
OF *THE LIGHTKEEPER'S BALL*

"Don't ever mistake [Coble's] for the fluffy romances with a little bit of suspense. She writes solid suspense, and she ties it all together beautifully with a wonderful message."

—LIFEINREVIEWBLOG.COM REVIEW OF *LONESTAR ANGEL*

"Colleen is a master storyteller."

—KAREN KINGSBURY, BESTSELLING AUTHOR
OF *UNLOCKED* AND *LEARNING*

LEAVING
LAVENDER
TIDES

Also by Colleen Coble

LAVENDER TIDES NOVELS
The View from Rainshadow Bay
The House at Saltwater
Point (Coming July 2018)
Secrets at Cedar Cabin
(Coming January 2019)

ROCK HARBOR NOVELS
Without a Trace
Beyond a Doubt
Into the Deep
Cry in the Night
Silent Night: A Rock Harbor
Christmas Novella (e-book only)
Beneath Copper Falls

SUNSET COVER NOVELS
The Inn at Ocean's Edge
Mermaid Moon
Twilight at Blueberry Barrens

HOPE BEACH NOVELS
Tidewater Inn
Rosemary Cottage
Seagrass Pier
All Is Bright: A Hope Beach
Christmas Novella (e-book only)

UNDER TEXAS STARS NOVELS
Blue Moon Promise
Safe in His Arms

THE ALOHA REEF NOVELS
Distant Echoes
Black Sands
Dangerous Depths
Midnight Sea
Holy Night: An Aloha Reef
Christmas Novella (e-book only)

THE MERCY FALLS SERIES
The Lightkeeper's Daughter
The Lightkeeper's Bride
The Lightkeeper's Ball
Alaska Twilight
Fire Dancer
Abomination (Republished
as *Haven of Swans*)
Anathema (Republished
as *Where Shadows Meet*)
Butterfly Palace

**JOURNEY OF THE
HEART SERIES**
A Heart's Disguise
A Heart's Obsession
A Heart's Danger
A Heart's Betrayal
A Heart's Promise
A Heart's Home

LONESTAR NOVELS
Lonestar Sanctuary
Lonestar Secrets
Lonestar Homecoming
Lonestar Angel
All Is Calm: A Lonestar
Christmas Novella (e-book only)

Leaving

LAVENDER

TIDES

A Novella

COLLEEN
COBLE

THOMAS NELSON
Since 1798

Leaving Lavender Tides

Published in Nashville, Tennessee, by Thomas Nelson. Thomas Nelson is a registered trademark of HarperCollins Christian Publishing, Inc.

Thomas Nelson titles may be purchased in bulk for educational, business, fund-raising, or sales promotional use. For information, please e-mail SpecialMarkets@ThomasNelson.com.

Publisher's Note: This novel is a work of fiction. Names, characters, places, and incidents are either products of the author's imagination or used fictitiously. All characters are fictional, and any similarity to people living or dead is purely coincidental.

Library of Congress Cataloging-in-Publication Data

Names: Coble, Colleen, author.
Title: Leaving Lavender Tides : a novella / Colleen Coble.
Description: Nashville, Tennessee : Thomas Nelson, 2018. | Series: A Lavender
 Tides novella ; 2.5
Identifiers: LCCN 2017060987 | ISBN 9781404106765 (hardcover)
Subjects: | GSAFD: Suspense fiction. | Christian fiction. | Mystery fiction.
Classification: LCC PS3553.O2285 L43 2018 | DDC 813/.54--dc23 LC record available at https://lccn.loc.gov/2017060987

Printed in the United States of America

18 19 20 21 LSC 5 4 3 2 1

For my beloved husband, Dave.
Every hero in my books is inspired by you in some way.

Chapter 1

The first time he saw her, he stopped and stared with his mouth open, absorbing the aroma of the flower lei around his neck. Hawaiian music floated through the hotel lobby like a movie track, and his vision narrowed until all he saw was her beautiful face framed by her black hair. Even from this distance he could see the vivid green of her eyes and the planes of her high cheekbones. He could almost feel the soft texture of her creamy skin and smell the scent of her, something sweet and wonderful for sure.

She was a vision from another world, and he wasn't sure she was real until she turned and looked at him. It was as if she could see straight into his soul, down to everything that made him who he was, and she loved every speck. They'd had some good times together, and he'd thought he lost her. This was his second chance to do it right, to hold her close and never let her go.

A porter came for her luggage, and she broke her gaze with him. With her luggage gone she glanced around with a smile that reached down and seized his heart. The sweet curve of her neck drew his attention when she tilted her head back to look at the ornate ceiling in the lobby. He'd kissed that neck many times, and he thought never to see it again, yet here she was. Tourists and hotel staff flowed past him as he stood rooted to the spot.

The love on her face took his breath away. A smile split his face and he opened his arms. He took one step toward her, then realized her smile wasn't directed at him but at another man. She didn't see him at all.

His smile fading, he stood staring after her as she walked away. He wasn't aware he'd crumpled the rose in his hand until blood dripped onto the floor from where a thorn had pierced his skin.

She'd see him—soon. She would remember the love they'd shared and would share again.

✤

The Honolulu sunshine warmed Shauna Bannister's skin as she stood at the balcony railing beside her new husband and waved at the crowd on the pier. A few clouds drifted lazily overhead in a perfect blue bowl of sky. The sweet aroma of the lei around her neck wafted to her nose and added to her sense of well-being.

Back home in Lavender Tides, Washington, the leaves would mostly have changed, and the October temperatures would be in the fifties instead of this wonderful eighties weather.

Zach's warm lips nuzzled her neck. "I have you all to myself for the next eight days."

A delicious shiver went up her spine, and she leaned against Zach with a contented sigh. "It sounds wonderful. I've always wanted to see Hawaii." She turned and peeked into the spacious suite. "This must have cost you the earth."

She still couldn't believe this wonderful man was all hers. His dark good looks attracted plenty of appreciative female glances wherever they went, but his blue eyes watched only her. Thoughtful, strong, brave, and committed were words that all described Zach Bannister, but his most admirable trait was his steadfastness. How he'd gotten to be thirty-three without being snagged by another woman was a mystery.

He took her hand and brought it to his lips. "The cost wasn't bad. One of the cruise line's bigwigs is one of my longtime customers. He gave me a great price."

She followed him into the penthouse suite and marveled again at the huge bed topped with crisp white linens accented with a pop of aqua. Spacious windows and sliding doors let the Hawaiian sunshine stream into the space and revealed an impossibly blue ocean. It was far from the cramped cabin she'd expected.

"As beautiful as this is, I want to see the rest of the ship. Let's go get some coffee."

"My thoughts too." He held open the door for her, and they stepped out into the hall and found their way to the deck with the coffee bar.

She looked around as he ordered them both black coffees. The casino machines faded to a dull roar as she noticed two older men staring at them from the casino next door. One was almost as round as he was tall with a balding head that gleamed in the overhead light. He was probably in his sixties. The other one had an aging surfer look with tousled brown hair streaked with blond like he might have worn it in the sixties. His tailored khaki slacks and crisp white shirt gave off an expensive vibe, and she guessed him to be in his midsixties as well. Both men were smiling as if they knew them.

The portly gentleman gave a half smile and waved as if he expected her to recognize him. When he approached her with the other guy behind him, she clutched Zach's arm. "Do you know these guys?" she whispered.

Zach turned around and a smile lifted his lips. "Otis, I haven't seen you in ages!" The two men shook hands, and Otis clapped Zach on the shoulder as he pumped his arm.

Otis drew the other man forward. "This is Raul Jackman. We met here in Honolulu a few days ago. Raul retired a few months ago after an impressive career in Silicon Valley. He's forgotten more about computers than I've ever learned."

Zach shook his hand. "Good to meet you, Raul. Zach Bannister. Otis was my favorite professor in college."

The tension drained from Shauna's neck and shoulders, and she stepped toward the men with her hand extended. "I'm Shauna, Zach's wife."

The aging-surfer guy reached for her hand first. "Raul Jackman." His smile widened. "Good to meet you, Shannon."

"Shauna."

His smile faltered. "Sorry, I misheard."

Shauna felt an instant pull toward the man. "It's nice to meet you." She shook Otis's hand too.

His blue eyes gleamed with appreciation as he took her hand. "You're a cute little thing, aren't you?"

She hated to be reminded of how short and petite she was. Shauna let him keep her hand until the handshake felt a little too personal, then pulled away with an apologetic smile. She didn't know him well enough yet for this kind of effusiveness.

"On vacation?" Otis asked.

"We're on our honeymoon," Zach said. "What are you guys doing here?"

Raul shrugged. "It's my retirement reward."

Otis looked away. "I'd always planned to take my wife to Hawaii for our thirty-fifth. She died six months ago, but I decided to come anyway."

Zach winced and clapped his hand on the man's shoulder. "I don't know what to say, Otis. I'm really sorry." He slipped his arm around Shauna in a protective embrace.

She felt incredibly selfish at the thought that she might not have Zach to herself this trip. His friend Otis obviously needed some support after losing his wife, and she should be glad they were there to give it, but the balloon of her anticipation suddenly deflated. This might not be the honeymoon she'd hoped for.

Chapter 2

*H*is *wife.* Zach's gaze lingered on Shauna's smooth tanned arms, bare in her vibrant turquoise dress. Her black hair was in an elegant updo that revealed her neck and shoulders and made her look a bit taller, which she probably liked. Her hands were in motion as she talked with Raul and Otis, who'd joined them for dinner. Crystal chandeliers glittered overhead, and the murmur of conversations around the dining room filled the air.

It was going to be a great honeymoon, and maybe they'd be able to let go of all the terror they'd gone through in the past month.

He realized Shauna and Raul were staring at him. "What?"

"Raul asked you a question three times." Shauna's green eyes held a teasing light. "Thinking about that bike ride in the morning?"

He grinned. "It's going to be fun."

"Getting up at three is not going to be fun." Her green eyes smiled at him over the rim of her water glass.

"Hey, that's five our time. I'm not on Hawaiian time yet, are you?"

"That's its only saving grace." She glanced at Otis. "What are you fellows doing tomorrow on Maui?"

"I thought about that Haleakala ride, but I'm not sure I'm up for that. I might sleep in, then head for the beach and snorkel, maybe take in a whale-watching excursion in the afternoon."

Zach focused his thoughts. "Sounds good. We're doing dinner at Leilani's on the Beach tomorrow night. Want to join us?" Shauna's smile dimmed. He should have kept his mouth shut, but he'd seen the loneliness in Otis's face.

Otis raised his brows in mock alarm. "That's okay. You guys are on your honeymoon. You need to hold hands and gaze at the sunset. I might cruise the bars and look for a cute tourist."

Raul let out a careless laugh. "All these couples make me want to have a woman on my arm too."

Saved by their good sense. Zach grinned. "Good luck, buddy."

Over dinner Raul had talked about all his travels. The man had made millions with a start-up dot-com business. He'd shown them pictures on his phone of him standing at a temple in India with his wife some years back.

Raul stared off into the distance. "We didn't go on beach vacations. She was afraid of water, and she much preferred cultural experiences. A new wife could never measure up to her."

Zach's gaze cut to Shauna. If anything happened to her, he didn't think he could ever remarry either. She was irreplaceable. But she'd remarried him after losing the love of her life, his best friend, Jack.

For a year they thought Jack had fallen accidentally while climbing, an event Zach blamed himself for. They'd found things were not what they seemed and that the danger was far from over. Together they'd obtained justice for Jack, and now the future was a bright ribbon in front of them.

The servers began to clear away the dessert plates, and Zach realized it was nearly seven thirty. People would probably be waiting for their table since the cruise line did freestyle dining. "Guess we'll head out of here."

Shauna rose as if she had been waiting for him to say that. "I wanted to go to the comedy show tonight, but I'm really beat. It's ten thirty our time, and I don't think I can stay awake for it."

And he was eager to have his bride all to himself. He took her hand and smiled at the men. "See you later, guys. Have a good evening."

A shadow passed over Otis's face but was quickly gone. "You too."

As they got out of earshot, Shauna rose on her tip-toes to whisper in his ear. "They probably wanted us to hang around with them longer. I just couldn't do it." She produced a big yawn and sighed.

He squeezed her hand. "Me neither. We need some time alone."

A blush made its way up her creamy neck, and she nodded. "We need to protect our time together. I don't want to get home and regret how we spent our honeymoon."

He kept possession of her hand as they made their way to the cabin. He locked the door behind them and saw a cute towel bunny on their bed. It guarded a sprinkling of chocolates. "They really know how to make us feel special." He scooped up two squares and handed one to Shauna.

His cell phone dinged with a message, and he dug it out of his pocket to glance at it. "We know your brother's name. It's Grayson Bradshaw."

Shauna had been searching for her brother and sister ever since she discovered they didn't die in an earthquake like she'd been told.

"Grayson, not Connor?"

"His new parents gave him the name. Since no one seemed to know who he was, they were free to name him whatever they wanted."

"It'll be hard to quit thinking of him as Connor." She lifted her head and smiled up at him. "I'm glad we have this time here first. It gives me a chance to roll around the different scenarios in my head. Like how will he react when we find him?"

"Let's try not to expect anything. It's going to be a shock."

She nodded. "I'm trying not to obsess about it. We have other decisions on our plate too. The upgrades to the airport have to be determined, and we've been talking about hiring another helicopter pilot if we have a baby."

Having a child was high on their list of creating the perfect life together. Her son, Alex, was five and a joy to both of them, but they'd love to have a child together. Shauna had inherited a good chunk of money from her mentor, and he had a hefty amount still in savings, but the ideas for expansion of Hurricane Roost Airport held challenges they'd have to work out.

All good reasons to keep this time for themselves. A lot of things would distract them once they left the cruise. He pulled her closer and found her eager lips.

✢

Zach's breath fogged in the frigid air at the top of Mount Haleakala in Maui. The tour operator had provided them with coats, but the blowing wind cut right through him. He kept his arm around Shauna, though it wasn't much protection from the cold.

"You doing okay?" he whispered in her ear. "I feel a little light-headed."

"Me too, but I'll be okay."

The parking lot looked like a volcanic moonscape filled with swirling fog that periodically parted to reveal people bundled in coats and gloves. The van had picked them up just before three in the morning to drive them to this spot just below ten thousand feet.

He caught his breath. "Look!" The sun burst over the horizon in a showy display of magical golden light.

The chatter of the other tourists fell silent as the sun put on a display that had been unfathomable when he'd first heard about it. The sun was *above* the clouds and painted them in a golden orange that took his breath away. Shauna's, too, for she gasped beside him.

Haleakala means "House of the Sun," and watching the sunrise burst out of the darkness explained the name. Legend said the demigod Maui had captured the sun and forced it to slow its journey across the sky to lengthen the day.

"It's unbelievable." Shauna slipped a cold hand into his.

"You're freezing."

"It's about time to start biking. That will warm us up."

Once the sun pushed into the blue sky, they piled into the van and drove down to sixty-five hundred feet, where the tour guides handed out bicycles and helmets. "Sure you're up to this?" he asked Shauna.

"I just drank a bottle of water. That will help this

headache that's starting." She shivered as she took possession of her bike, a sleek red one. "I thought this was a *tropical* honeymoon."

"Our steward told me this was an experience we would never forget. He was right."

The tour guide, a young woman with long black hair, waved for their attention. "We've had people killed on this road. Accidents are not uncommon, so I need you to pay attention. No gawking at the sights when you're going around hairpin curves or against oncoming traffic. Space yourselves out and be aware of what other bikers are doing."

Killed? He exchanged a long glance with Shauna. He'd never heard it was that dangerous, though he understood how accidents could happen with the volcanic outcroppings and rough terrain. He and Shauna were both excellent bikers, but he planned to keep her in his sight at all times.

Once she was mounted on her bike and pedaling down the mountain, he fell into place about four feet behind her. The view of green valleys and blue ocean invigorated him, and the last of his fatigue blew away. The way they'd go around a curve and seem to drive straight into a cloud was exhilarating.

The grade of descent went steeper as they approached a curve up ahead. He applied the brakes to avoid running into Shauna, but the grips went all the way down. He frowned and tried to slow again with the same result. The bike accelerated as he reached the curve, and he swerved to avoid Shauna.

"Sorry!" he shouted as he flew past her.

The wind rushed past his cheeks and down the neck of his jacket as the bike sped up as he came out of the curve. The grade down looked steeper yet, and he searched around for a soft landing where he could change out his bike, but jagged black lava lined both sides of the road.

He clutched the bike grips and looked ahead to where a truck was gearing up to lumber past in the intersection. If he was gauging the speed right, he would hit the side of the vehicle unless he did something.

He lifted both feet from the pedals, then began to use his sneakers as a brake against the pavement. The bike lurched to the right, but he managed to keep it from crashing into the volcanic shale along the shoulder.

He thought he heard Shauna shout, but the wind snatched away her words. Most of the group probably knew by now that he was in trouble. He dug his toes harder against the pavement, and the bike finally began to slow. The intersection drew near much too fast, and the truck driver hadn't noticed Zach was struggling.

He had to stop now or he was going to slam into the side of the truck. He dug in with his sneakers hard enough that the tops of his toes started to burn, then he set both feet down flat on the pavement. The bike rocked, then toppled over to his right. He put out his hand to catch himself, but his palm skidded in the shale, and his shoulder and cheek slammed into the rocks.

He slid in the loose rocks, then finally came to a stop near a large volcanic boulder. Pain exploded along his cheek and shoulder. His bike had landed several feet ahead of him, and the tires still spun as he lifted himself on his smarting elbows.

"Zach!" Shauna was at his side trying to help him up. "You're bleeding."

Wincing, he leaned on her and managed to stand. With every second he felt more scrapes and abrasions. "It could have been worse." He touched the blood trickling down his cheek.

The tour guide reached them. "What happened?" She handed him a bottle of water and began to rummage in a first aid kit.

"The brakes failed." He felt a little light-headed and leaned a bit on Shauna.

The tour guide blanched and looked over at his battered bike where the male tour guide was examining it. "That's impossible. We have them checked every night."

He stood still while she applied a stinging antiseptic to his elbow. "Someone evidently didn't check mine. The brakes failed completely."

His mouth in a grim line, the male tour guide rolled the bike toward the van. "The brake cable was cut."

Shauna's head came up, and her green eyes narrowed. "Cut?"

"Yeah, I don't understand it." The man hefted the bike onto the rack at the back of the van. "I'll run you down to the clinic to have you looked over."

Shauna helped him to the van, and he limped up the steps to drop into a seat. It wasn't the best start to their honeymoon, but at least it had happened to him and not to Shauna.

Chapter 3

The grass roof overhead and the sound of the surf a few feet away from their open-air table at Leilani's on the Beach in Whalers Village should have calmed Shauna's agitation, but she couldn't stop thinking about that cut brake cable. The server, a pretty Hawaiian woman, brought their pineapple-vanilla sodas and the ahi poke they'd ordered as an appetizer, then left them alone to enjoy the approaching sunset.

Shauna eyed her husband, who looked tanned and healthy in his blue Hawaiian shirt and khaki shorts. The accident had shaken her more than him. "How are you feeling?"

"Fine. A little sore but nothing major."

The clinic had treated his scrapes—stitching one cut—and let him go. It could have been so much worse. She already knew what it was like to lose a husband, and the thought of how close she'd come to losing Zach sent a shudder through her entire body.

He reached across the table and held her hand. "Don't look so worried, honey. I'm fine."

"Who would have cut that brake cable?"

"Maybe no one did. Things can wear out."

She lifted a brow his way. "Zach, you saw that cable. It was cleanly sliced in two. Someone would have had to take a cable cutter to it."

His chagrined expression spoke volumes. "I'd hoped you hadn't noticed."

"It was pretty hard not to see it must have been deliberate."

She loved the way he liked to shield her from life's harsh realities, but she wasn't a child. "Did the tour owner have any ideas?"

Zach took a sip of his soda, then scooped up some poke. "I tried to call him when I was waiting for an X-ray, but I didn't reach him."

"You'd think he'd want to make sure you were all right."

"The tour guide probably reported my mishap was minor."

Her gaze went out to the sea, now touched with gold and orange from the sunset. "We're here in paradise and having to look over our shoulders. I'd thought our honeymoon would be carefree, Cowboy."

He swallowed his bite of poke. "It's going to be fine, Fly Girl. Just a slight hiccup. It might have been someone who wanted to cause mischief and didn't care who got hurt."

"I don't like it."

In spite of his smile, she saw the worry in his blue eyes. It was clear that he didn't like it either, but knowing Zach, he wouldn't want to add to her worry by voicing his own.

A band began to play Hawaiian music as the server wound her way through the tables to bring them their scallops and Parmesan-crusted mahimahi meals. The twang of the steel guitar mixed with the softer ukulele, and the tense muscles in her shoulders relaxed.

The aroma of the Kula corn and Molokai sweet potato gnocchi made her mouth water. "I'm hungrier than I realized."

Zach picked up his fork. "We missed breakfast and lunch."

As they shared each other's meals, Shauna let her gaze drift over the patrons. There was a sweet couple who might have been celebrating their fiftieth wedding anniversary and people in their twenties who sported matching sunburns.

She was finding it hard to relax. Zach could have died today, and she would have been widowed. Again. She couldn't bear to go through it again.

She stared at her handsome husband. "You're not allowed to die."

His expression went tender. "I know it was traumatic for you to see that today. Don't think I'm not sympathetic to your fears, but you have to let go of them. God's got me, you know. And you."

"I thought he had Jack." The words burst out of some well she hadn't known existed. A well of fear and distrust.

"He does."

Zach's gentle reminder brought tears to her eyes. Jack wasn't lost. "It's hard to remember this life isn't what it's all about."

"I know. It's hard for all of us." He reached across the table and gripped her hand in his strong fingers. "I don't know what I'd do if I ever lost you or Alex. I guess it's easy for me to talk when I've never lost a spouse, but one thing I do know is that God would carry me."

She looked down at the table and nodded. "I don't know why we're getting so morbid on our honeymoon. We have years and years together ahead of us." The desperation in her voice made her wince, and the way his fingers tightened told her he'd noticed.

"I love you, honey. Let go of that fear, okay?"

"I'll try."

Who would have cut the bike's brake cable and why? Just for kicks to see what some random person did, or was there more to it? She needed to let go of her paranoia and fear, but she wasn't quite sure how.

☙

Zach had to nearly stop the Jeep to navigate the hairpin turn on the Hana Highway. The vistas of cliff and blue water below were breathtaking, and the scent of flowers filled the air. Shauna undid her seat belt and stood to take a couple of pictures out of the topless vehicle. It was a repeat of many other pictures taken so far.

She sat back down, buckled up, then took a sip of the coconut lemonade she'd gotten in the last town she couldn't pronounce. The mingled flavors of coconut and lemon made her sigh with satisfaction. She put her drink in the holder and smiled at Zach. "You realize this is called 'The Divorce Highway.' We haven't argued even once."

Both of his hands gripped the wheel. "If we survived nearly getting murdered by criminals a month ago, we can survive this."

He had a point. "You're not getting rid of me that easily. I caught you fair and square."

His hand squeezed her bare knee. "I think it's the other way around."

Warmth spread out from his touch. Too bad they weren't in their cabin. She put her hand on his. "It's been a great day." She glanced to her right. "Oh, we're at the bamboo forest. I really want to do that hike." She slurped down the last of her lemonade.

"Me too." He parked along the side of the road. "Looks like an entry here. According to the guidebook, we just look for an opening, then head back in there to the main trail that will take us down to the stream."

She unbuckled and grabbed the camera. "Should we put up the top and lock the Jeep?" She sprayed an essential-oil bug spray on her bare skin.

He squinted at the sky. "It could rain, I guess. I'll put it up just in case. We're taking everything with us."

She waited as he secured the top and shouldered the backpack with their food and water. She sprayed him down with repellent too, and they set off. The bamboo forest went gloomy a few feet in, and the air felt several degrees cooler. She paused to crane her neck up to the impossibly tall bamboo and watched the leaves sway in the breeze. The stalks bumped together, making an almost musical sound. In spite of the beauty, the place felt a little claustrophobic.

Zach pointed to a well-beaten path. "There's the trail."

They began to follow the footpath. No other hikers were in sight, which surprised her. Maybe they came in at a different spot. The back of her neck itched, and she rubbed it. The humid air pressed in like a moist, hot towel. They made their way down a treacherous, muddy slope and finally stood at the edge of an inviting pool of water filled by a beautiful waterfall.

"Let's stop and have a snack and some water." Zach shrugged out of his backpack and unzipped it. He opened a plastic container and offered her a brownie in a baggie, then handed her a bottle of water.

"Thanks." As far as she was concerned, this was far enough. Insects buzzed around her, and she was itchy and hot already. She wasn't about to be a spoilsport. This hike had been the first thing on Zach's list. It was already two though, and by the time they hiked back to the fourth and fifth pools, it would be late in the afternoon. Luckily the boat was docked in the harbor all night, and they could return at their leisure.

Zach's eyes were bright, and his grin spread across his face. "This is awesome, isn't it?"

"Gorgeous," she agreed. And it was beautifully tranquil. The sounds of birds mingled with the lullaby of the waterfall. Maybe she could do this and enjoy it.

Zach bit into his brownie and it disappeared in three bites. He pulled out another. "I'm famished."

"You had two before we left the boat." She nibbled on hers. It had an odd taste she wasn't fond of. "I wonder if they should have been refrigerated."

"I don't think so." He looked at hers. "You're not going to eat it?"

She shook her head. "You can have it if you want."

He reached for it. "I don't know why I'm so hungry. We just had fish at that food truck an hour ago." He swallowed the last brownie in two bites, then chased it down with half a bottle of water. "These are yummy. I don't know why you don't like them."

She stretched out her legs to enjoy the bake of the sun on her skin. "Let's sit here for a few minutes. It's so peaceful." And she wasn't looking forward to that upcoming hike.

He scooted over closer and embraced her. She nestled in the crook of his arm and laid her ear on his heart. This was the life, snuggled up against the man she loved so much. What was a little hike? Time slowed and she listened to the thump of his pulse and his even breathing. Her eyelids drifted shut, and she let herself relax.

It seemed only seconds since she'd closed her eyes when she felt him cough. Her lids flew open, and she sat up. The sun was lower in the sky, and several other hikers sat along the pool with their legs dangling into the water. Maybe their voices had awakened her.

That thought flew out of her head when she looked at Zach. His skin was almost blue, and his eyes were big. "What's wrong?"

"I think I'm going to throw up." He bolted to his feet and darted into the bamboo. "My lips feel a little numb too, and I'm so hot."

She heard him retching and dug out a paper towel from the backpack. She wetted it and took it to him. "Here, honey."

"Thanks." His voice was shaky, and he wiped the back of his neck with the damp towel, then swiped it over his mouth. "I feel pretty lousy. If you don't mind, we should probably go back to the ship."

"I knew those brownies weren't quite right. We should get you to the doctor."

Chapter 4

Zach didn't know when he'd felt so horrible. The wind lifted the damp hair from his forehead and brought with it the sweet scent of plumeria. The smell heightened his nausea. No matter how much he rinsed out his mouth, he couldn't get rid of the awful taste from vomiting. He shivered, and his stomach continued to roil as he lowered himself to the soft green grass beside their parked Jeep. Sweat poured down his face, and his head throbbed.

Worry lining her face, Shauna put a warm hand on his forehead. "I don't think you have a fever. Could it be food poisoning? I thought those brownies tasted funny."

"The brownies tasted fine, so maybe it's the flu. I don't think I've thrown up since I was a kid." His voice sounded weak, even in his own ears. Way to go. Nothing like looking like a feeble fool on his honeymoon.

"I'm going to take you to the hospital. You're green." She helped him to the Jeep and opened the door.

He practically fell into the passenger seat. "I think I'm going to need a bucket or something."

She opened the backseat passenger door and emerged with a plastic bag. "Will this do?"

He took it. "Let's leave the window open. Maybe the fresh air will help."

She nodded and went around the front of the vehicle to get behind the wheel. He drew in deep breaths to beat back the nausea. When the Jeep didn't start, he looked over at her. "What's wrong?"

"It won't start. It won't even turn over." She tried again, and there was only silence.

It was his job to check the battery cables and the engine, but it took every bit of strength he had to shove open his door and get out. More sweat broke out on his forehead with the effort to swallow down the bile crowding the back of his throat, and he could barely feel his lips and tongue.

He unfastened the latches and lifted the hood. The stench of gasoline and oil hit him in the face, and he nearly retched again. He took a quick swig from the water bottle in his hand, and the nausea subsided.

He leaned over and studied the wires and belts. Wait, the battery cables were disconnected, their metal ends gleaming in the sunlight. How had this happened? It couldn't have been accidental.

"Hey, brah, need a hand?"

He turned to see a young Hawaiian with long black hair and a sumo wrestler build leaning out of an old red pickup. It looked like the same guy who had waited on them at the food truck where they'd had lunch.

"You wouldn't happen to have any tools, would you? The battery cables are off." For a moment Zach wondered if this guy or his companion in the passenger seat had pranked him.

The man smiled and nodded. "Easy fix. I've got a toolbox in the back." His appreciative glance darted to Shauna, then back to Zach. He turned his truck off in the middle of the road and hopped out, then reached behind the seat for a battered red metal toolbox.

His friend got out too, and the two conferred about what to do. A few minutes later the cables were connected, and the engine purred to life as soon as Shauna turned the key in the ignition. Her beautiful face lit with a brilliant smile, and the young men poked one another and grinned.

"Can I give you something for your trouble?" Zach pulled out a hundred-dollar bill, but both men shook their heads and moved toward the truck.

"Just giving you a little bit of aloha, brah," the driver said. "Pass it along to the next person in trouble."

"Mahalo." He called his thanks after them as they pulled away, their tires spitting gravel as they left.

His stomach heaved again, and he rushed to the ditch, but all he could manage were dry heaves. What was he going to do about this? His legs were shaky as he climbed into the passenger seat and fastened his seat belt.

"We're going straight to the ER." Shauna's tone brooked no objection.

He was okay with that. The way he felt, it wouldn't hurt to have a doctor examine him. He'd had mishap after mishap, and there's no way the battery cables came loose accidentally.

❧

The ER room was small and austere, and the odor of antiseptic stung Shauna's nose. She sat on a chair close to Zach's bed and watched him rest. His color was improving, though he was still a little green. An IV drip dangled from his left arm, and the monitors beeped quietly at the head of his bed. He'd tried to smile at her, but his lips didn't move right. It was almost as if he'd had dental work and his face was numb.

The ER doctor, an attractive Asian woman of indeterminate age, stood on the other side and studied her computer tablet. Dr. Chang's kind eyes and gentle manner put Shauna at ease.

The doctor laid down her tablet and darted to the door and called for the nurse. "We need to pump his stomach. And get a ventilator in here!"

Pump his stomach? Ventilator? Zach was looking worse by the minute. Terror clawed at her insides, and Shauna backed out of the way as nurses and technicians flew into the room and began to work on him. He looked even worse by the time they'd pumped his stomach. His breathing seemed fine, but the ventilator was nearby just in case.

When the doctor finally stepped back from the bed, Shauna touched her arm. "What's going on, Doctor?"

"He's evidently eaten a puffer fish, Mrs. Bannister. Where did you eat lunch? Did he have fish?"

"He had a fish soup that was supposed to contain mahimahi. We bought it at a little food truck called Kai Bites. It looked clean and safe."

"It wasn't. Puffer fish is very fast acting. How do you feel?"

"I'm fine. I just had crab cakes, no soup. Is he going to be all right?"

"We'll know for sure in a few hours. If he survives the night, his chances are good that he'll be out of here in twenty-four hours. His symptoms aren't severe yet, so I'm hoping we got most of it pumped out. And his symptoms didn't appear for several hours, which is a good sign, too, as far as indicating a small amount was ingested. We'll give him activated charcoal and push fluids. We'll also be ready to support his breathing. That's all we can do. There is no antidote."

If he survives the night? This was a horror beyond comprehension. "You can't tell me he'll live?" She shook her head and backed away from the doctor. This couldn't be happening.

Dr. Chang reached toward her and laid her hand on Shauna's arm. "Let's try to stay positive. I'm hopeful since you brought him in so quickly. Is this an overnight port?"

"Yes, the ship doesn't leave Maui until tomorrow night."

"I'm going to send the health department over to the food truck. Unfortunately puffer fish is a delicacy to Asians, and they sometimes don't get all the poison glands out. I suspect that's what happened here." The doctor gave her an encouraging smile. "With the Lord's favor, you'll both be on that boat, so try not to worry."

Shauna wanted to believe the doctor, but the fear of losing Zach clawed at her chest. "I-Is there a prayer room here?"

The doctor's eyes were kind. "Of course. It's on this floor. Down by the elevator. Would you like me to ask the chaplain to stop by?"

"No, that's fine." Shauna bolted for the door.

Her legs trembled with weakness, and she struggled to hold back the sobs until she reached the prayer room, a small carpeted room with several chairs circling a small podium. A table held pamphlets, a Bible, the Torah, and the Qur'an. A crucifix hung on the wall, and several prayer rugs were draped over a quilt rack. A prayer kneeling bench was on the opposite wall.

She dropped onto the prayer bench and let the tears fall as she prayed for God to carry her. She wanted to demand for him to heal Zach, to demand answers, but all she could do was bow her head and lean into God's love.

Words wouldn't come even for prayers. God knew how she felt though, and that was enough in this moment. When she walked back to Zach's room, God's peace went with her.

Zach's color was better, and he seemed to be resting. One of the nurses had moved in a recliner for her, and Shauna curled up in it with a blanket the nurse had left. She couldn't close her eyes and had to watch Zach for any sign of breathing difficulties. Through the long afternoon and into the evening, she kept vigil over him.

At one point she tried to call his mother but didn't reach her. This wasn't the kind of news to leave in a voice mail, so Shauna just asked her to call when she had a chance. She reached Marilyn, her first husband's mother, who was keeping Alex, and asked her to pray. Marilyn promised to call the church and ask everyone to pray too.

Just after midnight Zach's eyes opened and he turned his head toward her. "Shauna?"

She leaped up and went to his side. "I'm here."

His warm fingers clasped hers. "I can feel my tongue and lips again. I think the poison is wearing off."

Shauna leaned over to kiss him. "Oh thank God. I've been praying constantly."

His hand cupped her cheek. "I wouldn't leave you for anything, Fly Girl. Not willingly."

"You'd better not." She straightened. "I'm going to get the nurse."

She darted for the door and fetched the head nurse, who assured them both that Zach was improving. Once the doctor came by in the morning, they'd be able to leave.

Chapter 5

Shauna felt like she could walk on the clouds by the time she got Zach settled in the suite on the ship. Insisting he felt fine now, he'd wanted to go out with her, but she ordered him to bed before heading to the buffet to get him some soup. She stepped out into the hallway, nearly mowing Raul over as he came around a corner. "I'm so sorry!"

"No harm done." His blond-streaked hair fell across his forehead, and he brushed it away. The aqua Hawaiian shirt he wore over khaki shorts deepened the color of his hazel eyes. "Are you okay? You look a little frazzled."

"I'm fine but Zach isn't." She told him what had happened.

She felt the sensation of the ship moving and realized they'd left Maui and were heading for Hilo on the Big Island. All she could do was pray that whoever seemed to be targeting them wouldn't follow them to the next island.

Raul's smiling eyes turned serious. "That's terrible. Is there anything I can do for him?"

"He's resting now, but thanks."

Raul glanced at his watch. "Look, you need to eat yourself. I'm supposed to meet Otis for dinner. Please join us. Then you can take Zach back some broth and pudding or something afterward."

Zach would likely sleep for a while, but she wanted him to have something to eat when he awoke. "Okay."

She followed him to the buffet line and grabbed a burger and fries. He opted for pizza, and they found Otis at a table near a big window. Raul quickly filled in his friend as they slid into the booth.

"You should have called us," Otis said. "We would have come to be with you. You shouldn't have had to go through this by yourself."

"I didn't have your numbers." The food aroma made her mouth water. She was hungrier than she'd imagined.

Raul frowned toward the buffet line. "See that guy? He's been watching you."

She shot a glance to her left and her neck prickled. "The Hawaiian one? He looks a lot like the owner of the food truck where we ate lunch yesterday. If he's working at the food truck, why is he on board?"

"I think I'll find out." Raul rose and approached the man.

Shauna shot surreptitious glances at the two men as they talked. The big guy had his fists clenched, and his frown deepened as Raul spoke to him. He stalked out of the dining room with an angry glance her way. Raul's lips were pressed together as he returned to the table.

"What happened?"

"I asked him how he could be working here and at Kai Bites also. He claimed he didn't work at the food truck and that he boarded this ship in O'ahu. I asked his name, and he wouldn't give it to me. I wanted to verify if he was really a passenger."

Could it have been a different man from the one she'd seen yesterday? Everything was such a jumble, she wasn't sure what to believe right now. "Maybe it's a different guy."

"And maybe it isn't," Raul said.

"The brake cable was deliberately cut. That much we know. The puffer fish was an unhappy circumstance no one caused though. I don't see how they could be related."

Otis frowned. "Someone could have deliberately slipped puffer fish in Zach's soup."

Her stomach clenched. "I hadn't thought of that. Why would anyone do that? The doctor said this sometimes happens."

Otis shrugged. "Why would anyone cut a brake cable?"

Shauna's eyes burned, and, appetite gone, she turned her gaze onto her plate of food. Nothing about this trip was turning out as she'd expected. She couldn't let Zach see her discouragement though. He'd blame himself, and it certainly wasn't his fault.

Raul touched her hand. "You okay?"

She swallowed down the boulder in her throat. "I'm fine. Just tired. It's been a long day, and I didn't get any sleep last night." She forced herself to take a bite of her hamburger, though it had no more taste than the sand on the beach. She swallowed and picked up a fry. "Thanks for keeping me company."

Otis put down his fork. "It's our pleasure. What's on your agenda for tomorrow?"

"We're docking in Hilo, but it depends on how Zach is feeling. If he's strong enough, I'd like to see the banyan trees and Volcanoes National Park, then take a tour over to see Kilauea. I want to see the lava falling into the ocean as it creates more land. It's supposed to be spectacular. How about you guys?"

Raul took a sip of his soda. "We might take in the hike at the national park to see the waterfall and the observatory over lava vents. I don't do helicopters very well. You're a chopper pilot, aren't you?"

She nodded. "I'd like to fly one over the landscape, but it would cost the earth to rent one." Although she could well afford it since her inheritance from Clarence, it felt much too lavish. They'd have expenses for the airport expansion too, and Alex would be going to college someday.

"I suppose so. Besides, the pilots here know where to go. I'd guess the heat rising from the volcano could make for some tricky flying."

"That's probably true." She finished half of the hamburger, then grabbed the plate of fries. "I think I'll take the rest of this back to the room. Zach might be up by now."

"Don't forget to pick up food for him."

She smiled across the table at Raul. Several women from the table next to them had glanced their way, and she knew the men could find some female companionship if they wanted. "You're both good friends. Thanks. Have a good day on your hike tomorrow."

Otis looked to her left at the flirtatious blonde Shauna had noticed. "I plan to."

Smiling, she took a detour past the buffet to scoop up things for Zach, then headed for their suite. She reached the large staircase and saw the big Hawaiian guy again. Her smile vanished, and she practically fled to their cabin.

❧

Zach felt a thousand times better when he opened his eyes to a darkened room. Through the open sliding door to the balcony he could see the shore lights glittering on the water. The murmur of laughter and voices drifted to him as he swung his legs over the side of the bed and stood.

No nausea, no numbness. Thank the good Lord for that. And thank God it had happened to him and not to Shauna. After all his adventures—BASE jumping, skydiving, rock climbing—he was laid low by something as simple as fish soup.

His head felt surprisingly clear, and thoughts of a big slice of pepperoni pizza crossed his mind. The doctor had said clear liquids only though, so pizza was out. The glass of water on his nightstand would have to do for now, so he swallowed down the lukewarm liquid.

He was rummaging in the fridge for a Sprite when the lock on the door clicked and Shauna came in. Sprite in hand, he closed the refrigerator door and eyed the bowl in her hand. "Looks like you brought me some strawberry goo. Did they have any pizza-flavored Jell-O there?" The sundress she wore showed off her toned arms and terrific legs, and her mother's Haida hummingbird necklace gleamed against her skin. "You look much tastier than pizza though."

She laughed and put the food on the table. "You must be feeling better."

"Back to normal, I think." He scowled at the broth. "That doesn't look nearly as appetizing as a pizza."

"You can have pizza tomorrow."

"Promise?"

"As long as you don't throw up again. It's all on your head, babe." She looked out toward the balcony where the sound of music echoed across the water. "Let's go sit out there. I'll grab your food."

"Too late." He was already wolfing down the Jell-O, which was like eating nothing. It wasn't going to do much to fill the empty place in his belly.

He followed her out the door to the deck chairs on the balcony. They'd left port, and the shore lights were pinpoints in the distance. Someone on board was playing a steel guitar for a male singer. They didn't sound professional, but the music lifted his spirits. He could see the dim outline of several figures on a far beach, and someone had lit a bonfire. The shadows thrown by the huge moon overhead added to the beauty of the ocean scene, and he even smelled sweet flowers in the air.

Shauna set the glass of broth down, then went to lean against the railing. "It's so beautiful here. I love Hawaii."

He set his empty bowl down and went to join her. "You're beautiful. I'm glad we could experience this together. I want to bring Alex back sometime. He'd love learning to dive."

She punched him. "Not yet, Cowboy. And even when he's ten, I'd have to think about it pretty hard."

That sweet fragrance he'd smelled was on Shauna.

Totally luscious. He slipped his arms around her, and she leaned back against him so he could rest his chin on her head. In spite of the trials that had hit them since they boarded, there was nowhere he'd rather be right now than with his beautiful wife tight in his arms.

"I had dinner with Raul and Otis, and we saw a guy who looked like the man running the food truck."

He stiffened. "He was a local. What would he be doing on the ship?"

"That's what we wondered. Raul went to talk to him, and he claimed he boarded the ship in O'ahu. He looked pretty mad at being confronted."

"Are you sure it was the same guy?"

"I'm not sure, no. I could have been wrong."

Someone on the beach laughed, a crazy hyena giggle that made him grin. Kids having fun. "No idea what his name is?"

"He wouldn't tell Raul."

It was strange all right. Zach didn't know what to make of it or even if it affected them at all. And maybe it wasn't even the same guy.

Shauna shifted in his arms. "We could go for a stroll around the ship and see if we stumble into him."

They could, but he'd much rather stay here and

inhale the sweet scent of jasmine on her skin. He nuzzled her neck. "Sure you want to go out?"

She laughed and turned in his arms to nestle closer. "I might be able to be talked into staying in."

He slid his lips up her neck to kiss her jaw. "I can be pretty persuasive."

"Don't I know it." Her soft breath whispered against his face, and her lips met his.

Chapter 6

He stood outside the suite door and wished he could break it down and rescue his lady love like her white knight on a horse. Whisk her away from her boorish husband, who practically held her prisoner. He never seemed to let her go anywhere without him. How long was she going to put up with that nonsense?

He'd had his mole plant a device in the morning flowers yesterday. He knew exactly what they were planning to do at every moment. The volcano might be an interesting place to take her home, but he had to get Bannister out of the way. The man was aggravatingly tenacious, but he couldn't really blame him. The problem was she belonged to him, not Zach. They'd been meant to be together from the beginning of the world. She'd been made for him, and he didn't intend to let her go.

It might take some time for her to remember her previous life, but it would happen. He was sure of it.

Keoni had nearly blown things today. The idiot had wanted more money, and he'd arranged to meet him after dinner. Keoni was gone now, and good riddance.

The steward he'd been paying to help him, Gretzky, shot him a glance as he passed the suite door. He tightened his lips and looked away. It was important that no one saw them together. The man had proven to be invaluable. He'd hired someone to arrange for the bike accident and had paid Keoni for puffer fish poisoning, though it had cost him dearly. He wouldn't have minded the money so much if his scheme had worked, but Bannister was still alive.

He turned his back on Gretzky and headed for the outside deck. Some fresh air would clear his head so he could determine what to do next. He only had a few days to get it all planned out. Why hadn't Bannister died yesterday? The plan had seemed foolproof. Maybe he'd just have to grab Shauna out from under Bannister's nose. But first he had to figure out where to keep her until she remembered who she used to be. That could take a while, and he didn't want anyone stumbling into their nest before she regained her memory.

Maybe when they got to Kona he would find the right opportunity. The Big Island contained many remote spots. He just had to find the right one.

❧

Water dripped from the leaves and illuminated the intricate pattern on a spiderweb. The forest's shades of yellow, reds, blues, and vivid greens almost hurt Zach's eyes, but he'd take it since he awoke feeling so much better. This place was like being in another world saturated with more color than the eye could take in. They'd docked early this morning in Hilo on the Big Island, then picked up the rental car to explore Volcanoes National Park. He hadn't expected a rain forest.

He pulled rain slickers out of his backpack. "I guess this really is a rain forest." They paused long enough to put on the protective plastic.

"Are you sure you're up to a hike?"

"I'm great. Raring to go."

She pulled up the hood on her slicker. "I've never

seen anything like that lava tube. The ceiling was way over our heads." She shuddered. "It was creepy though, even with the lights strung around. I kept expecting to see spiders or snakes come crawling out of the dark."

"There aren't any snakes in Hawaii."

"I keep reminding myself of that."

Zach couldn't wait to share the surprise he had for her. His gaze scanned the parking lot as they neared. Maybe they were here now. He spotted a tiny Asian woman and a big Hawaiian guy. Though he'd never met the Oanas, he recognized Annie's flashing dark eyes from a picture his friend had sent him. Zach had sent the Oanas a wedding picture so they'd recognize Shauna and him.

Annie turned their way and smiled. "You have to be Zach and Shauna."

Shauna stopped and glanced up at Zach. He smiled his reassurance. "We are. Shauna, this is Annie and Mano Oana. Annie is a volcanologist, and Mano is an oceanographer. They're going to take us on a tour of the lava fields."

She gaped and stretched out her hand. "How wonderful! I can't thank you enough."

Mano's smile lifted his face. "We hear you're a

chopper pilot, so we managed to snag a helicopter for you to fly. We can direct you on where to go. We can land out near the active lava flow and take as long as you want to look around before flying back."

"Thank you, thank you!" Shauna hugged him. "I was just telling a friend last night how much I'd like to fly over the lava fields myself. I can't wait."

Zach grinned at the excitement in her voice. Maybe his arrangements had made up for the first couple of days of problems. His phone rang and he glanced at the screen. The doctor was calling to check on him evidently. He turned away and walked a few steps from the group so they could chat.

"Dr. Chang, good morning."

"You sound chipper," the doctor said. "No lasting issues?"

"Nope. I had broth and Jell-O for dinner, lots of water in the night too. I woke up feeling completely normal."

"I'm glad to hear it, especially after I got those samples of the soup back from the lab." Dr. Chang cleared her throat. "The main pot of soup was fine, totally uncontaminated, but the puffer fish had to have been in the soup."

His chest tightened. "I don't quite understand."

"I'm concerned your soup was deliberately contaminated with puffer fish."

"You think someone tried to poison me on purpose?"

"I think it's possible," she said, her voice careful.

He cut his gaze to his wife, so beautiful with her black hair hanging down her back and her slim, tanned legs showing from under her shorts. He loved her with everything in him. Who would want to hurt him?

"What should I do?"

"Perhaps you should talk to the police. At the very least, be vigilant. Maybe it was coincidental, some person who thought it would be fun to make a random vacationer sick, though it could have easily killed you. I thought you should know what we discovered."

"Thank you for that. Let me know if you find out anything else."

"Of course."

The call ended, and he turned off the screen.

"Who was that?" Shauna asked.

"Dr. Chang." He glanced at the Oanas as he relayed the doctor's warning.

Alarm widened Annie's eyes. "There's no known

antidote." She studied Zach's face. "You are very fortunate to have survived it."

Shauna had gone pale as she listened. "By itself the fish poisoning could have been random, but when you add the cut bike cable, things change from random to more likely targeting you specifically, Zach."

Annie glanced from her to Zach. "Bike cable?"

He told them about biking on Sunday. "We made excuses for that accident, too, and went on with our honeymoon. It looks like maybe we should have reported it to the police."

"Should we do that now?" Shauna asked.

Zach glanced at the other waiting couple. "I'm not about to spoil a day I've planned for weeks. Let's go enjoy the adventure. I can report it all tonight when we get back. We'll be with Annie and Mano all day. Nothing should go wrong today."

"You're sure?" Mano asked.

"Yep. Lead on, brah."

The big guy smiled and indicated the big white van. "Let's head out to the helipad and get the chopper. It will take about fifteen minutes to fly to our landing spot. You won't ever forget this experience." He glanced from Zach to Shauna. "Either one of you have asthma or lung problems? The acid in the volcano can be hard on the lungs."

"Nope, we're both healthy." Zach took Shauna's hand, and they climbed into the back of the van.

As they pulled away, Zach glanced back at their rental car. A figure seemed to be crouched beside it. He closed his eyes and opened them to find no one there. He was starting to imagine boogeymen everywhere he looked.

Chapter 7

Shauna loved the feel of the helicopter controls in her hands. This baby was responsive and lovely. She swooped over treetops an impossible shade of green and saw winding black rivers of hardened lava that had cut their way through the expanse of the beautiful island. She hovered over verdant valleys with waterfalls and glimpsed the beautiful blue of the ocean in the distance.

Shauna couldn't help but shoot up a prayer of thanksgiving for the beauty of creation spread out for them to enjoy. It truly took her breath away. Annie directed her to fly out over the vast expanse of black lava fields interspersed occasionally with spouts of steam. She flew the chopper toward a plume rising off the ocean where the hot lava dripped into the waves. The acrid smell burned her nose and throat.

Annie was in the passenger seat beside her, and the men were in the back. Annie pointed out the lava river that held glimpses of red in it. "That flow is called Kamokuna or 61g. It started in May 2016, and since late July 2016, it's been creating new land as the lava falls into the water. It's not been a danger to any towns since it's followed another flow's previous path. See that flat spot next to the large rock? We can set down there and hike over for pictures. There's a skylight I'd like to show you."

Shauna nodded and began to hover in for a landing. She set the chopper down with hardly a bump, then shut off the engine. She took off her helmet with the headset. "I'm glad we wore sneakers today. I wouldn't want to step out on that with sandals."

Annie released her seat belt and opened the helicopter door. "This area is pretty safe if you know where to stand. I came out this morning to make sure."

Birds swooped overhead, and Shauna caught the salty tang of the ocean mixed with the acrid stink of sulfur. She glanced at Zach and saw him looking at his phone. He was grinning and did a fist pump.

She stepped over to him. "What's going on?"

"Just more info about your brother."

A wild pulse throbbed in her throat. "Tell me."

"The dad was in the Navy, and they moved to Okinawa right after they adopted him."

"He's out of the country?"

"We're not sure yet. This is just the start of figuring out where he is. Take a look at the picture."

She looked at the photo on his phone of a little boy sitting on a woman's lap. Her chest compressed, and she couldn't catch her breath. "That's Connor!"

"It's Grayson now, but yeah, I was sure too." He draped his arm around her and pulled her against him. "We're close, Fly Girl. We're going to find him."

"No sign of Brenna yet?"

He shook his head. "But I'm not giving up. I'm going to find her."

Warmth spread up her neck. She loved this guy so much. Kind, thoughtful, gentle yet strong, and so loving. She laid her head against his chest. "What did I ever do to deserve you?"

"I'm the lucky one." He gave her a final squeeze. "I think they're ready for us."

She turned to see Mano and Annie smiling their

way. "Sorry." She told them about losing her siblings in an earthquake twenty-five years ago. "And Zach has found out what happened to Connor. We should know in a few more days where he is."

"How wonderful! I pray you find them both." Annie gestured to her right. "The skylight I wanted to show you is this way."

As Annie picked her way over the uneven lava field, Shauna noticed her limp. "Are you okay? Did you sprain your ankle?"

Annie turned with a somber face. "Safety is critical out here. I didn't heed my own advice some years ago. A lava bench gave way, and my right foot went into molten lava. The doctor thought the limp might go away, but it still appears when I'm walking on uneven ground. So if at any time I say to stop, listen to me."

Shauna swallowed. "I'm so sorry." Her and her big mouth. She couldn't imagine the pain of hot lava touching her skin. Did she really want to do this? If a volcanologist was burned out here, maybe it was a stupid idea.

Annie's expression softened. "You'll be fine. We're not getting that close. I was retrieving lava samples when this happened. I'm not taking any chances with the two of you, so don't worry."

Shauna curled her fingers into the steady strength of Zach's grip. "Okay."

They followed Annie and Mano across the rough, hardened lava. The stench of fumes burned her lungs, and Shauna quickly understood Mano's caution about coming out here with lung problems.

Mano held out his arm. "Don't go any closer. You can see it from here."

They were standing on a hump of lava around what appeared to be deep hole. Shauna leaned over a bit and peered down. It was like looking into a portal to hell. The deep-red glow below was molten lava, and the hardened forms surrounding it were twisted into bizarre shapes that brought her heart to her throat. Some of them looked like tormented faces. It was like a scene straight out of Dante's *Inferno*.

She held Zach's hand in a death grip. "I don't like this place." What if Zach fell in? The thought of that made her mouth go dry.

Annie's studied absorption with the skylight vanished, and she nodded. "We can go now if it's too much. I know being this close can be terrifying. We're safe up there though. Where we're standing has been hardened for years and goes down many feet."

"I think I'm ready to go too," Zach said. "Can we see the lava flowing into the ocean?"

"Sure can. It's this way," Mano said.

They followed their guides toward the water, but the fumes weren't getting any better. Maybe this had been a bad idea all the way around.

❧

In spite of waking up this morning feeling great, the hike across rough ground in noxious fumes had Zach's energy flagging by lunchtime. His chest burned and his legs ached. Shauna was a trooper though and had kept pace with Annie and Mano with a smile on her face, at least once they were away from that skylight. It had freaked him out too.

They sat munching sandwiches and swigging water on a ledge overlooking the newly forming land. With the hiss of steam and the sound of the ocean as a backdrop, he couldn't think of when he'd experienced a more interesting meal. Although the fumes in the air made his sandwich taste like sulfur.

"We'll head back after we eat." Mano balled up his plastic bag and stuffed it in a paper sack. He peeled an apple banana and popped it in his mouth in one bite.

"I'm kind of addicted to those apple bananas," Zach said. "I'll have to look for them at home."

Annie shook her head. "You won't find them. They're only available here because of the banana fungus. We can't export them." She frowned and shaded her eyes with her hand. "What's that idiot doing?"

Zach followed her line of sight and saw a Zodiac-type boat getting too close for comfort to the plume from the hissing lava. The guy was looking up at them and not paying attention to how close his craft was drifting into danger. "He's going to get sucked in." He leaped up and gestured with his arm for the guy to steer away.

The guy frowned, then looked over at the plume. Seemingly in no hurry, he started his engine and jetted out of danger.

"You get all kinds out here," Annie said. "Nearly a tourist a week dies while in Hawaii. People get really careless and don't take the warnings seriously. That guy shouldn't have been anywhere near this spot."

"Well, let's get started back. You two need to be on

board the ship in time to depart for Kona, and it will take us an hour or more to hike back to the helicopter," Mano said.

An hour. The thought of it brought a hard knot to Zach's stomach. What he really wanted to do was stretch out here on the hard ground and turn his face to the sun. A half hour nap would do wonders for his depleted energy.

Shauna slipped her hand into his. "You look a little pale, Zach. We have time to rest a bit." Before he could assure her he could make it, she turned toward Annie. "I think we have time to take a rest. How about we let him take a quick nap in the sun while we do a little more exploring?"

"I know, but I'm fine, really."

Annie looked him over. "I think resting is a great idea." When he started to object, she smiled and shook her head. "I'll take good care of your wife, and we won't go far." She shrugged out of her backpack and dropped it to the ground. "Use this to rest your head. There's a fairly smooth spot here." She moved the backpack to a smooth shelf of black. "Close your eyes for twenty minutes."

The thought was like a glass of ice water on a scorching day. It wasn't too hot out to sleep in the sun either. The temperature hovered at around seventy-five. "Just a few minutes. And don't go far."

"I'll stay with the women every minute," Mano promised.

Zach stretched out and rested his head on the back-pack. Bliss. He closed his eyes and knew nothing more as he dozed.

He jerked upright sometime later, his heart a jack-hammer in his chest and his mouth dry. Was that a scream he heard? Maybe Shauna had fallen off the cliff into the water. He bolted to his feet and looked around wildly.

He struggled to draw a breath past the panic. He raced for the blue expanse of water. They had to be there. He stood on the edge of the cliff and looked down into the sea, foaming white as it threw itself against the black lava rocks.

No one was out here. He heard no voices and saw no figures. His panic mounted into a tsunami. Cupping his hands around his mouth, he shouted, "Shauna!"

Then he saw them. They'd gone east a ways to where the lava delta sloped down to the water. Huge waves crashed up and nearly touched their feet. She hadn't turned to look at him. The sound of the waves and the hiss of the lava would drown out his voice. His heartbeat resumed its normal rhythm, and he picked his way across the delta to where they stood.

"I think we should move back," Mano said. "The waves are getting bigger as the tide rolls in. A rogue wave could sweep us straight out to sea."

Satisfied they were backing away, Zach glanced around and caught a glint of something on the ocean. That Zodiac again, and it looked to him like the guy was watching them with binoculars. Wait, he had some of his own in his backpack.

Zach retraced his steps and yanked his binoculars out of the front pocket. As he began to focus them, he heard the distant sound of the motor revving, and the boat sped away. He caught only the glimpse of a broad back covered in a Hawaiian shirt.

Chapter 8

The ship slowly moved away from the Hilo port. Shauna and Zach sat on the deck and waved to people on shore. Now that they were away from the volcano, the tension she'd felt all day slipped away. There was no good reason for the fear she'd experienced, but she'd been on edge the entire time.

She wasn't about to tell Zach that, not after he'd gone to all that trouble. He'd been quiet too.

"Anything new on Connor?"

He'd changed into khaki slacks and a Hawaiian shirt for dinner. His dark hair still gleamed from a quick shower as he shook his head. "I don't expect to hear much for a few days at least. It's probably going to take some time, but we're getting close."

"You're quiet tonight. Tired?"

"A little." He took her hand and laced his fingers with hers. "I'm glad to have some downtime with my best girl."

She studied his expression and noted the cloud of worry in his eyes. "I think it's more than being tired. Did you call the police about the puffer fish poisoning?"

"I did. They are investigating, but they warned me it probably wouldn't be possible to track down the culprit, though they are interviewing everyone who had access to the soup."

"Someone at the food truck had to have done it."

He nodded. "The police advised me to be aware of my surroundings and contact them if I see anything suspicious."

She couldn't think about what could have happened anymore. Still keeping his hand, she rose. "I'm starved. Ready for dinner? Our reservation is in fifteen minutes."

"Yep." He stood, and they headed for the dining room. "I think Raul and Otis are meeting us too. Raul texted me that he had a date too."

She'd hoped to have Zach to herself, but at least Raul would be occupied with this new woman in his life. "Did he say who it was? I saw a couple of women flirting with them last night."

Zach showed her a picture on his phone of Raul with the blonde she'd seen last night. "That's her, but I'd thought Otis was interested in her. I hope it works out."

Zach shrugged. "Holiday romances don't usually pan out. There's not enough time."

"Oh, and how many holiday romances have you been involved with, Mr. Bannister?"

He grinned. "Well, just one when I was in college and spending spring break in Florida. What was her name? Kristy, Kayleigh?" He shook his head. "See, I can't even remember. And anyway, all women are just a forgotten haze when I look at you."

She elbowed him. "Charmer. If I wasn't so sure you meant it, I'd be all over that."

He slipped his arm around her waist. "You know it's true. You've spoiled me for any other woman."

Her smile still curved her lips when they stepped into the dining room. The hostess seated them a couple of tables over from where they'd been the last time. The place buzzed with excitement and happiness. Everyone must have had a good time today.

Raul was already there with his blonde admirer, and Otis was on her other side. He waved at them.

Shauna smiled at them and extended her hand to the woman. "I'm Shauna."

The woman's fingers barely grazed hers. "Elaine Cooney."

She looked older than Shauna had thought last night, probably forty-five or so. Her blonde hair looked freshly dyed, and there were lines around her brown eyes and mouth.

Shauna settled in the chair Zach pulled out for her and ordered an iced tea. "So what did you guys do today?"

"I had a massage," Elaine said. "I think Raul and Otis went to see the volcano."

"So did we, but we had a helicopter, so we got up close and personal." It wasn't until she thought about the packed tour the two men had done that she realized how lucky she was that Zach had planned such an awesome outing for them. And here she'd spent most of the day wishing she hadn't been there.

She reached for Zach's hand under the table and squeezed his fingers. "I'd like to go snorkeling tomorrow in Kona. I hear there's no runoff and you can see for a hundred feet."

"I'm going to go diving." Raul reached for a roll and buttered it. His hair was carefully combed, and he had on a tie and sport coat tonight.

Zach reached for a roll too. "I'd love to take Shauna diving sometime. She's never learned. If we'd had time, I would have had her do her book training before we came, then done a checkout dive here."

Otis put down his menu. "Maybe she could do a shallow recreational dive. Some companies allow that."

"I wouldn't feel comfortable letting her do that. I'm a big believer in the proper training before attempting something like scuba. She's too precious to me to risk."

Raul looked down, and Shauna wondered if he was thinking of his dead wife. "Did your wife dive too?"

Raul shook his head. "She was afraid of water too, a little like you."

"I'm not really afraid of it," Shauna said. "It's just I always remember I have a son to raise. I wouldn't want to do anything risky and leave him without a mommy."

"You have a son? I didn't realize," Otis said.

"I'll have to show you his picture." Shauna sent a smiling glance her husband's way. "Zach is an awesome dad to him. Life couldn't be better."

Elaine flagged down the waiter. "I need some wine. All this happily-ever-after stuff is making me crazy."

Shauna refused to let the woman's catty remarks dim her joy. Tomorrow was going to be a great day.

⚜

Zach had rented them a convertible, and he glanced over to watch Shauna lean against the headrest. She gave a sigh of pure contentment. "It's another gorgeous day in paradise. Look at that blue sky." She breathed in deeply. "And smell the plumeria in the air."

The sweet fragrance of flowers swirled in the gentle trade winds that stirred the palm trees along the road. Nothing could go wrong today. They'd slept in and had a late breakfast, and it was nearly lunchtime before they picked up the car and headed out to explore.

She turned a smile on Zach. "I feel like such a slug to let you plan everything. What are we doing today?"

He'd wanted to plan it all and surprise her. "I thought we'd have lunch in downtown Kona, then do a little shopping, maybe get some shaved ice in the middle of the afternoon. I have reservations at Ulu Ocean Grill.

It's supposed to be great. Tonight I thought we'd do the manta ray snorkel trip. I booked us on the 6:15 p.m. departure tour, so we'll do an early dinner if that's okay with you."

"It sounds like a wonderful way to spend the day."

Keeping his attention on the road was hard when she looked so beautiful. She wore white shorts and a red top that made her dark hair gleam. She'd put her hair up in some kind of twisty knot, and the wind teased tendrils loose. He'd like to set the rest of it free.

He found a parking space and squeezed around a group of tourists who weren't paying attention to traffic. His phone dinged with a text message when he turned off the engine. He glanced at it.

"Anything about Connor?"

He smiled at her eager voice. "Nothing yet. The airport expansion has run into a snag with permits. I'll have to make a call to straighten it out." He spied a jewelry store across the street. "Go browse through there, and I'll join you when I'm done. Don't look at the price—just pick out something you love." He got out and came around to her side of the car to open the door.

"Ooh, that's dangerous." Her green eyes sparkled.

He kissed her, enjoying the sweet taste of her lips. "I

like living dangerously." He watched her sashay into the store, then walked across the street to the seawall overlooking the water and placed the call. The backdrop of the ocean's beauty and the sound of the waves gave him a strong sense of well-being. Once he got this work straightened out, he'd concentrate on making this a day for them to remember forever.

A dog, tail wagging, wandered over as he placed the call, and he petted it absently. Apollo and Artemis, his two rottweilers, would be missing him, and he couldn't wait to see them.

By the time he finished arranging the permit, his stomach was growling. The wind brought the scent of coffee and sweet rolls to his nose, but they both needed something more substantial. Maybe they'd visit the Mexican place down the street.

Zach glanced at his watch. He'd been on the phone for half an hour. He rose to join Shauna, then heard a faint cry. Shading his eyes with his hand, he looked out to sea and saw a hand go up in the waves. Was someone drowning, or were kids just playing around on their surfboards?

He looked around for a lifeguard but didn't see any. Without thinking, he kicked off his flip-flops in case he needed to dive in. Had he imagined someone shouting for help? He studied the rollers crashing toward him and still saw no one. Wait, there was that hand again. He vaulted over the three-foot seawall and jumped into the water and swam out into the big rollers.

He paused, treading water, then saw a young woman floundering in the waves. In seconds he had her in a lifeguard hold. "Stay calm. I'll get you to shore."

The undertow was treacherous, and he fought against it with her body dragging them back even more. He was getting winded and fatigued. Glancing at the shoreline, he saw a spit of land he thought he could reach if he used the undertow to his advantage. He struck out in that direction, and minutes later they both lay gasping on shore.

"Zach?"

He looked around and saw Shauna with her mouth open in a horrified expression. She rushed to his side. "You're bleeding."

He looked down at the gash on his leg. He must have cut it on coral or a rock. "It's not as bad as it looks."

Shauna knelt beside him and put pressure on the bleeding cut. "It's going to need stitches."

Another trip to urgent care and more treatment.

At this point maybe they should just go home. But he didn't want to spoil Shauna's dream trip.

The young woman sat up and coughed up some seawater, then swiped her long blonde hair out of her face. "I don't know how to thank you. I would have drowned. I fell off my board on that last wave, and it hit me in the head. I was so dazed I couldn't swim right."

"You hurt anywhere?" he asked.

She shook her head. "I don't think so. I swallowed some water, but I'm okay."

Shauna rose and held out her hand to him. "We need to get you to a clinic for stitches."

Zach was used to being the one who responded in a crisis, not the one who was constantly needing help. He didn't like it one bit.

Chapter 9

I don't really want to go without you." Shauna looked out the side of the boat at a beautiful sun dipping into the ocean. The colors were glorious as the darkness began to push the blue from the sky.

The other snorkelers were busy putting on fins and cleaning masks, but she would rather sit here by Zach and watch the action with him. The salt would sting his wound, but even worse, the cut might seep blood and attract a passing shark.

"I want you to go. I've heard it's something not to be missed. I've already paid for the videographer, and I can enjoy it vicariously through you when we watch the movie. You'll only be gone half an hour." He reached down and grabbed her fins. "Here, put these on. They're going to get you in the water any minute."

It had been too late to get their money back. She'd feel terrible if he spent all that money for nothing. "All right, but I don't have to like it."

He grinned. "I'm going to have some Kona coffee and stay warm while you have fun. There are snacks here too, and I plan to take advantage of them."

He sounded upbeat, which helped her decide to go along with the plan. "Don't go near the side of the boat. I don't want you falling in."

His smile widened. "I'm staying put. I have to use those lousy crutches anyway." He gazed at her. "You look fabulous in that new bathing suit."

He'd bought her a new tankini in a deep iridescent-green color. She smoothed the fabric over her hips. "I think you're a little prejudiced."

His gaze smoldered as he looked her over. "I don't think so."

Her cheeks heated, and she adjusted her mask on top of her head, then bent down to kiss him. "I'll be back in a flash."

"I'll be watching."

She was the fifth one in the water and swam over

to hang on to the surfboard as directed. The surfboard had a window in it so the snorkelers could look down through the dark water to the floodlights on the sea-bed. Divers swam to and fro in the light, and she nearly gasped when she saw the majestic shapes of the manta rays join them. She let go of the board a moment to duck underwater with her mask and camera. She snapped as many pictures as she could before she needed to grab another lungful of air.

The other snorkelers were exclaiming over the amazing site as well, but there were so many it was hard to see through the fins, so she let go of the board and swam a few feet away to take more pictures. The manta rays almost looked like angels gliding through the water with their wings flapping lazily. It was a sight she'd never forget.

She emerged for another gulp of air and treaded water while she caught her breath. If only Zach could see this. He'd love it. He should have been down there with the divers.

She took a deep breath and was ready to plunge her mask into the water again when she felt a hard tug on her leg. Her head went under, and she turned to see a diver fully covered in a wetsuit hauling her away from the lights. It was too dark to see his face, but he was pulling her toward the shore about 350 feet away.

She fought to free herself, but he was so much stronger than her that she didn't even slow him down. She was too deep to use the snorkel, and her lungs burned with the need to breathe. Then he shoved her out of the water and clapped his gloved hand over her mouth, dislodging the mouthpiece attached to her mask.

"Breathe," he hissed in her ear.

Her lungs were clamoring for oxygen or she would have defied him and dived back underwater to get away, but she had to have air. She took in big lungfuls through her nose. Before she could struggle again, he dragged her underwater and swam toward the rocks again.

The sea was black ink, terrifying and disorienting wherever she looked. She had to get away from him and swim back to the boat for help, but her efforts to free herself seemed puny against his superior strength.

When she thought she'd pass out from lack of air again, he shoved her head out of the water again and commanded her to breathe. This time she inhaled more slowly so he couldn't tell as well when she had a lungful of air.

"Breathe!" He shook her a bit.

She forced herself to continue to take the short, shallow breaths that seemed to displease him. She squinted through her mask, but it was foggy, and she couldn't make out his features in the dark.

Someone shouted from the boat offshore, and his grip slackened momentarily. She took that brief moment and wrenched free of his grip, then swam for all she was worth underwater and back in the direction of the boat. She could only pray the night would hide her down here under the waves.

When her burning lungs could take no more, she popped her head up and glanced back but didn't see him. She dove again and began to see a faint light in the distance. When she emerged from the water again, she was near the boat. The surfboard and snorkelers were gone, and she heard the welcome sound of Zach yelling her name.

"Here, I'm here!" She swam to the ladder and emerged from the water to fall into his arms.

❧

Zach couldn't settle after the police left them off to board the ship. He paced the balcony outside their suite as the lights of Kona faded into darkness. Around them the sounds of the ship came to life—laughter, music, the distant murmur of conversation. Guests would be enjoying dinner and the nighttime shows, but he was as on edge as a soldier facing enemy gunfire.

Someone was targeting them. Specifically. And he'd nearly lost Shauna.

There was no doubt about that in his mind at all. He watched Shauna in her deck chair. She wore a pensive expression as she watched the Big Island fade into the distance. This hadn't been the honeymoon he'd planned, and that ticked him off. Instead, some maniac seemed out to destroy their happiness. But who? And why?

A knock came at the door. Zach opened it to a steward holding a large vase overflowing with flowers that obscured his face and revealed only a thick tuft of bright red hair. He tipped the man, then shut the door and carried the arrangement to the dining table.

Shauna had followed him in. "These are beautiful, Zach, thank you!" She plunged her face into the fragrant blooms of plumeria and inhaled the sweet aroma.

"I didn't send them." He studied the card and his gut clenched.

You've finally come back to me, and you're as beautiful as ever.

Shauna tried to see over his shoulder. "Who sent them then?"

"It doesn't say." He handed her the card.

She took a step back and shuddered. "That's really odd, Zach."

He checked the envelope and saw *My Beloved* written in a flowery script on the outside.

Zach's frown deepened and he shifted. "I think I'll go down to the flower shop and see if they know who sent these."

"I'll go with you."

After all the danger they'd experienced back in Lavender Tides, it was no wonder they were both on edge. He prayed that's all it was.

They went down the hall to the wide, scarlet-carpeted stairs and made their way to the area with shops and services. They passed jewelry stores, clothing shops, an Internet café, an art gallery, several chocolate and sweet shops, but no flower shop.

Zach flagged down an employee, a young woman

dressed in a white uniform. "Could you tell me where the flower shop is located?"

She produced a perfunctory smile. "I'm sorry, sir, but we have no flower shop. Flowers must be ordered at least a week before sailing."

"But someone just brought flowers to our cabin. We didn't order them. How can we find out who sent them?"

She directed them to the guest services desk, but fifteen minutes later, they were no closer to finding the mystery sender. According to the ship records, no flowers had been ordered or delivered.

Zach kept his hand on Shauna's waist and looked around at every passing stranger. "I don't like this. I didn't recognize the steward, did you?"

Shauna shook her head. "I didn't get a good look. The flowers were so massive they covered his face."

"Maybe it was on purpose." He hugged her. "I don't want you going anywhere without me, Fly Girl. Something seems really off about this."

"I'm not planning on letting you out of my sight, Cowboy."

❧

Shauna had changed into a black, red, and white sundress with a wrap to guard against the breeze. She patted the deck chair beside her. "Come sit down. It's not the first time we've faced danger together, and we'll figure it out. Until now we hadn't been sure what was happening."

"We still don't know." He let himself be coaxed over to sit beside her. Taking her hand, he tugged her toward him, and she rose to settle on his lap. "I don't think I could go on if I lost you. You had to have been scared."

"Terrified." Her breath whispered against his neck. "All I could think about was how devastated you and Alex would be if I'd drowned." She sat up and looked at him. "Here's the thing though—he wasn't trying to drown me. It was more of a kidnapping attempt than anything. He kept bumping my head above the waves so I could breathe, then he'd strike out with me toward the shore again. I don't think he wanted to hurt me."

Still holding her hand, Zach stroked her palm with his thumb. "The things that have happened to me are likely from the same guy who tried to take you."

She nodded. "So let's look at everything. The flowers are a weird development. It's like someone is obsessed with me, but you're the one who's nearly died twice."

"You sure you haven't seen anyone you recognized?

Maybe an old boyfriend from high school who has changed a lot?"

She dug her fist into his stomach. "I'm not *that* old!"

He grinned. "Hey, he might have lost his hair early or something."

Her gaze grew thoughtful. "What if it's someone who just saw me and I'm his type, you know? You see it sometimes in the movies—a guy gets obsessed with a woman. That's the only thing I can think of. I mean, there is *no one* here I knew from a long time ago. I have a great memory for faces."

He nuzzled her neck. "You're great at everything." Having her in his arms soothed his fears, but only a little. He had to keep her safe and not let her out of his sight ever again.

Who was after them? Nothing made any sense.

He reluctantly lifted his lips from her soft skin. "Okay, let's go over what we know. No one can tell us who delivered the flowers. Possible answers to that are the guy brought them to our door himself after borrowing a uniform, or he hired a steward to bring them."

She nodded. "We could talk to stewards we see and ask about it in a nonthreatening way, maybe even offer a reward for anyone leading us to who brought the flowers. If it's a steward, he might be able to tell us who hired him. If it's someone obsessed with me, maybe he wants you out of the way."

"But how did he carry out the deeds? How would he know which bike I would take?"

"Maybe he paid someone to make sure you got that bike. The bike company employee might not even have known the cable was cut. He could have given you the bike unaware it was dangerous."

He reached for the bottle of water on the table and took a swig. "Okay, possible. Then there's the food poisoning. That's a lot more problematic. How would he know you wouldn't eat the soup, too, and get sick?"

A frown furrowed her brow. "Didn't I mention something about fish soup sounding awful?"

He had a dim memory of that comment. "Yes, I guess you did."

"And then there's my attack. I only know it was a man, and he was strong. It was too dark to see his face or any identifying marks." She slipped off his lap. "Let's go get some dinner. At least we have some direction on what to check out."

He feared it wouldn't be enough to lead them to the lunatic, but they had to try.

Chapter 10

After dinner Zach decided to make a systemic search of the starboard side of the ship where their suite was located. He guessed the stewards and butlers had specific duties in adjacent rooms. The first few they stopped and talked to were polite enough, but every time he asked about a flower delivery, he got a blank stare and a shake of the head. One referred him to guest services where they'd gone first.

Shauna's black hair was falling out of its updo, and she looked a little frazzled. "This feels a little hopeless."

Zach glanced at his phone. "It's nearly eight. Let's head to our room, and we can ask any steward we encounter on the way, but we won't go down any random hallways."

"Sounds good. I'd like to veg out on the deck for a while. There's a beautiful moon."

"I can't think of anything I'd like better." He took her hand, and they went up the stairs to their deck.

A steward in a black uniform exited a cabin ahead of them on the left. Zach thought he might have seen the man before. When the steward spoke politely, Zach detected an Indian accent.

Zach stopped and smiled. "Busy time for you."

"Yes, sir, it is. May I help you in some way? I am at your service always." The man's friendly smile widened.

Zach looked at his name tag. Sal Chopra. "Sal, I have a few questions if you have time."

"Of course." The man's relaxed pose didn't indicate he needed to hurry away.

Zach decided to take a different direction with his questions. "I would guess the employees are always looking to make a little extra money."

Sal raised a black brow. "I am very satisfied with my salary, sir."

"But a little extra never hurts, does it? Do you know of anyone who would want to make a hundred dollars delivering some anonymous flowers? Maybe a steward supporting a family who needs some extra?" He knew many of the employees came from other countries where parents and siblings were dependent on money sent back home.

Sal locked gazes with him as if searching for the truth behind the questions. "There are a few employees like that. However, I am happy to assist you for no charge."

"Someone delivered flowers to our suite a little while ago. They weren't ordered through guest services. We'd like to talk to that delivery person and see who hired him. Would you know who we might talk to? We'd just like to thank him."

Shauna took a step closer. "It's our honeymoon, and someone was very thoughtful."

Sal went silent for a moment as if contemplating what he should say. "There is a steward who works this deck. He's from Belarus and is supporting his widowed mother and three younger siblings. He might know something."

"Could you ask him to stop by our suite?"

"I can ask, but he might be afraid he's in trouble."

Shauna brushed a strand of hair out of her eyes. "He's not in trouble. We won't talk to any ship management about this. That's why we are asking privately. We wouldn't want to get anyone in trouble."

"I will see what I can do."

"Could you tell us his name?" Zach asked.

"I would rather not until I know he's willing to speak with you." Sal's large brown eyes held an apology. "I hope you understand."

"That's fine. Tell him I'll give him a hundred dollars if he comes to talk to us. He won't be in danger of losing his job."

"Yes, sir." Sal glanced down the hallway. "If there's nothing more you need, I should get back to work."

Zach stepped out of his way. "Of course. Thank you for your help."

Sal smiled and moved past them to slip into another cabin. Zach took Shauna's hand, and they went down the hall to their suite. Sal must have already been there because a towel rabbit was in the middle of the bed with chocolates. The large suite was spotless, and the refrigerator had been restocked with goodies and drinks.

Shauna slid open the sliding glass door, letting in the distant sound of laughter and the lapping of waves against the ship. "I'd take some water if you want to grab it and come out here with me."

"Sure." Zach took two bottles of water from the fridge and joined her on the sizable balcony.

She was already stretched out in one of the turquoise lounge chairs. The moon was huge in the sky and glimmered on the sea as the ship plowed through the waves on its way to Lihue. The shimmer of ship lights reflected off the water too, and the scene was almost magical.

Zach handed her a bottle of water, then dropped onto the chair beside her. "I'm not hopeful the guy will talk to us."

She uncapped her water and nodded. "Even a hundred dollars might not sway him. This job is probably a godsend for him and his family. He might not be willing to risk it, even though we assured Sal he wouldn't get in trouble."

"And the poisoning was clearly a murder attempt. The stalker would have had to pay a lot of money to convince someone to do that."

Shadows gathered in her green eyes. "I can't lose you, Zach."

"You won't."

"I'm not sure what to investigate next."

"Maybe we should just go home. I can't lose you either."

She shook her head. "It's only two more days, and

I love it here so much. We'll be extra vigilant. What do you have planned for tomorrow?"

"I'd arranged for us to camp out on the Kalalau Trail. I've already notified the ship we won't be arriving back tomorrow night but will be back before we sail back to O'ahu the next morning." He reached over and took her hand, then kissed it. "It's one of the most beautiful spots in the world. Though I think right here with my gorgeous wife is better than anywhere else." He tugged her off her chair and onto his lap.

※

With only two nights left to execute his plan, he'd almost begun to despair, but Bannister couldn't have chosen a better place for this to work. He had the perfect cave all picked out and had taken in supplies earlier this morning. Food, water, sleeping bags, and extra clothing for them both. This time of year the tour companies didn't run. He'd have the place all to himself. And Shauna, of course.

He had everything ready by two when the rental car pulled into the parking lot. It was hard to miss her beautiful black hair in the open-air vehicle. He stood in the shadow of a large tree and watched them haul out their supplies. She danced around with excitement, and he had to bite back a chuckle. He loved her exuberance so much. That hadn't changed at all. She would soon remember everything.

But what about Bannister? He was stubbornly hard to get rid of. He should have died of food poisoning. That ride without brakes should have sent him straight over a cliff. Other people had died biking down Haleakala. How had Zach managed to escape?

But did he have to die? Once his beloved recovered her memory, she wouldn't want to go back to him. They could disappear to their new life, and he'd never find them. His lip curled, and he clenched his fists at the sight of Bannister dropping a kiss on her mouth. He'd had all he could stand of the man's liberties with the woman who belonged to *him*. It would be over soon though.

Was there a way to end Zach's life out here? If the man would get in the water, maybe the ocean would do the job for him, but he doubted Shauna would let Zach try to swim in those rough seas—even if he wanted to. His gaze drifted to the Na Pali spires to his right. He had no gun handy, and even though he had a knife, Bannister was no wimp. Killing him wouldn't be easy.

No, it was too late now. He'd just have to go with the plan. Once she realized she belonged with him, she'd settle down.

Chapter 11

Shauna stood exulting in the ferocious pounding of the waves on the shore far below. Her leg muscles felt quivery from the hike along the Hanakapi'ai Trail, but the views had been outstanding. The blue of the ocean and the vivid greens of vegetation in the valleys literally took her breath away. They'd even seen the outline of the coral reef protecting Ke'e Beach.

She tucked her hand into the crook of Zach's elbow. "This is magnificent!"

Zach pointed out the trail winding down to the valley below. "Let's camp by the stream and cross it tomorrow. I'd hoped to get farther, but the stitches are pulling a little. I haven't been able to move as quickly as I'd like."

She'd noticed him limping a little for the past hour and had tried to get him to stop, but he'd wanted to press on. "Let's just camp here. We don't have to climb down to the valley. We can camp right here, then return in the morning after you've rested."

"I really don't want to give up."

"I'm tired too." She knew her husband, and only concern for her would make him stop.

"You're just saying that. I think it would be great to stick our feet in the stream and get out of the wind for the night too. It's not that far."

"Okay, but we're stopping at the stream and going back tomorrow. I don't think I can hike the Kalalau Trail all the way."

He nodded, and she knew he saw right through her ruse, but as long as he didn't push on tomorrow, she didn't mind. They hiked down to the stream, a clear, beautiful river with big boulders. She immediately sat on a boulder and took off her hiking shoes to plunge her hot feet into the clear water. She could see the beach across the stream, and the inviting blue of the ocean tempted her to go now, but she wanted Zach to rest his leg.

He dropped the tent and cooler. "Where do you want to set up?"

The wind teased strands of black hair out of her ponytail. "Somewhere out of the wind? Maybe there." She pointed out a protected site.

"You got it." He hauled the supplies to the spot and began to set up the tent.

She watched his practiced movements. "You've done this before. I can't even remember the last time I put up a tent. Probably when I was in the Navy."

"We should take Alex sometime. He'd love it."

She helped him by holding a pole here and there, but he had the tent constructed in a few minutes. He put the cooler inside, then stood back and looked around with his hands on his hips.

His bare legs below his swim trunks were tanned and strong. "You've gotten some sun this trip." Her own suit was under her shorts and top, but she didn't plan on swimming at the beach. "I think we should stay out of the ocean. I've read it's dangerous to swim here."

He looped his arm around her waist and drew her in for a kiss. "People have died here crossing the stream when it's flooded. They've been swept out to sea too."

She shivered and leaned against his chest. "What do we want to do now?"

"Let's go for a stroll along the beach. Maybe we'll find a sunrise shell."

"Wouldn't that be great? I think we'd have better luck in the morning though." The sunrise shells were rare and usually only found at sunrise after a big storm. She didn't expect to find a golden beauty.

The sun beat down on her shoulders and heated her arms. The muscles in her legs ached from hiking, but she didn't mind. Not with Zach's fingers laced with hers. They crossed the stream and picked their way through the rocks to Hanakapi'ai Beach, a beautiful golden crescent of sand with waves pounding the rocks and shoreline.

Zach stared out at the sea. "It would be great to take a dip in the ocean, wouldn't it?"

She eyed the massive rollers pounding the shoreline. "Great wasn't quite the word I was looking for. Terrifying might be more apt."

He smiled and led her to a rock and leaned against it, then pulled her to him. "I wanted to wait to tell you until we reached the beach, but we've found Connor's location."

She gasped and turned in his arms to face him. "You mean, you actually know where he is?" He'd taken a call about an hour ago on the satellite phone he'd rented, and she had assumed it was something to do with the building project.

He nodded. "He's a civilian with the Coast Guard and is stationed in Washington State. He's an investigator."

Her breath came fast, and she felt light-headed. "You mean we can see him when we get home?"

"He's on leave at the moment, visiting his parents in Hope Beach."

"Where's that?"

"The Outer Banks in North Carolina, but he's not due back for three weeks."

"Oh, Zach, that's so long. Maybe we could call him."

"I think it would be best to tell him face-to-face." A teasing smile lifted his lips. "I know my wife pretty well, and I knew you wouldn't want to wait that long. I changed our flight home and booked us one out of Honolulu to the Outer Banks. We should be on his doorstep in another three days."

Three days. She didn't know whether to dance or cry. She cupped his face in her hands. "You are absolutely the best husband. I can't believe you've done this."

His blue eyes smiled back at her. "Anything for my

beautiful bride. It's been a pretty traumatic honeymoon for you. I'm hoping this will wipe away all the bad stuff."

"It hasn't been bad. We've been together, and that's all that matters."

He laughed. "Keep saying that and maybe we'll both believe it."

She wrapped her arms around his neck. "I wouldn't change a thing. Well, other than you being practically killed several times. But you're fine now. We're both okay, and I'm going to see my brother for the first time in twenty-five years."

Her vision blurred and her throat tightened. A year ago she'd thought her brother and sister were both dead and that she would be alone when her dad died. Now her life had changed dramatically. First of all, she had a new life with Zach. That was amazing in itself, but to have two siblings practically rise from the dead was a miracle. Brenna might be harder to find, but Shauna had faith in Zach. He wouldn't give up until he found them both.

She gave him a lingering kiss and inhaled the spicy aroma of his aftershave. "Let's eat our tuna and settle in for the night. I can't think of anything I'd rather do than share a sleeping bag with you."

"I brought marshmallows and chocolate bars to make s'mores over the fire. That might keep you awake awhile."

"Who said anything about sleeping?" She took his hand and led him toward the tent.

❧

The moon was so bright it penetrated the thin material of the tent, and Shauna found it hard to sleep in spite of the lulling effect of the surf outside. Zach's light snoring stirred her hair, and she snuggled closer until her bladder situation became urgent enough that she had to get up. She eased out of the sleeping bag and took a peek at her phone. Two in the morning.

Zach cracked open one eyelid. "Okay?"

She set her phone back down. "Just going to the bathroom. I'll be right back." She grabbed a small shovel and a roll of biodegradable toilet paper.

"I'll go with you," he mumbled.

"I won't go far, and I've got the flashlight."

She wasn't sure he'd listen to her, but his eyes drifted closed again. Luckily, he'd only been half awake. She slid her feet into her flip-flops and opened the tent's flap. The sound of the surf in the distance made her turn and look at the moon glimmering on the whitecaps as the big swells foamed against the beach. If only she had a camera to capture the sight, but she hadn't even grabbed her phone.

She turned toward the seclusion in the trees, then hurried across the sand into the scrub. With the moon so bright, she didn't need to flip on the flashlight, but she didn't want to come across a cane spider. She hadn't seen one yet, and she didn't care to.

Several other tents of campers were here, so she decided to cross the stream to a more secluded area. The cold water against her feet and ankles brought her more fully awake. She reached the other side of the stream and found a private area. After relieving herself and shoveling dirt over the toilet paper, she paused to enjoy the beauty. A shooting star streaked across the sky, and she made a quick wish on it to find her siblings, then added a prayer that would do way more good than wishing on a star.

Thankfulness welled up, and she blinked back tears. God had given her so much more than she deserved. She'd faced hard times this past year, but he'd worked it out for her good in ways she couldn't fully grasp.

A sound drew her attention. It was something like a roar of wind or water. The surf maybe? She turned back toward the stream and saw a huge wall of water barreling down the streambed toward her. She turned and darted away before the flash flood could reach her. They'd checked the weather before they set out today, but a storm must have blown through in the mountains. They'd been warned to be careful at the stream, but she hadn't expected to actually have to deal with a flash flood.

Now what? It wasn't safe to cross and probably wouldn't be for hours. Zach would be worried. She squinted in the moonlight to see if he'd exited the tent to look for her. She'd have to reassure him that she was fine and not to attempt to cross, even with the rope strung across the water.

It was going to be a long night with no sleeping bag or tent. She glanced around for a place to settle. Maybe against a tree where she could lean her head back and sleep a few hours. Wait, was someone here? She wheeled toward the sound of feet crunching on sand, her breath hitching in her chest.

The figure that emerged from the shadow of trees was familiar. "Raul, I didn't know you and Otis were going on this hike. I'm so glad to see you. Got an extra sleeping bag? I'm trapped over here."

His smile gleamed in the moonlight. "I sure do, but I have something better. I brought an inflatable raft, and we can cross over in the ocean. Zach will be worried if you stay over here."

"I didn't think landing on this beach was allowed. How'd you even get it here?"

He shrugged. "It's not legal, but I did it anyway." He jerked his head toward the beach. "Money always talks. I just hired someone to bring it in for me by boat. It's just down on the beach. Come with me, and I'll run you over. It will only take a few minutes."

She followed him across the rough ground to the sweet little beach. While the beach was beautiful, the water pouring out from the stream churned the ocean. "Looks like we'll have to go offshore a little ways to get past the flood."

"I've got a good motor on this thing."

His inflatable raft was on launching wheels and moved easily across the sand. He paused with his feet in the surf. "Climb in, and I'll finish launching."

She clambered up into the raft and settled at the bow. "I'm in."

He shoved the boat deeper into the water, then climbed in and started the motor. The sound of the surf muffled the roar of the engine, but the motor was up to the task, and the boat quickly puttered out to sea. It was only after they were out in the waves that she realized he couldn't get her to the other side from here.

"It's no use. We might as well land and get comfortable for the night."

He didn't seem to hear her. Wearing a slight smile, he steered the boat away from the beach and farther west.

"Raul, we need to go back."

He shook his head. "I've got everything planned, Shannon. Just sit down and enjoy the ride."

Shannon?

She'd barely registered his words when he rose and plunged a needle into her arm. Stunned, she stared at her arm, then at him. "Raul? What's going on?"

Her voice wobbled, and then her vision blurred. She couldn't make her tongue form any other questions before her lids became too heavy to hold open. Her chin sank onto her chest, and the world went dark.

Zach cracked open an eyelid. Wait, he'd wanted to go with her outside. Shauna couldn't have been gone longer than a few minutes. He struggled out of the entangling folds of the sleeping bag and stumbled to the tent opening. The roar of the waves filled his head, and the moon was so bright it made him blink.

His horrified gaze took in the water thundering down the riverbed where there had been a clear stream just an hour ago. "Shauna!" She wouldn't have gone near the flood, would she?

He cupped his hands around his mouth. "Shauna!"

Nothing moved but the raging stream. He shouted her name again, but he doubted she'd be able to hear much over the sound of rushing water.

He never should have let her go alone.

In the flashlight's beam, he saw footprints, small ones, down to the water's edge. "Shauna!"

When she didn't answer, he ran for the tent and grabbed his satellite phone. He dialed 911 and told the dispatcher his wife was missing. The woman reassured him she was likely fine, just across the stream before it had flooded, but he knew it was more than that.

He plunged into the events of the past week. "Check with Maui police. Two incidents occurred there. And the Big Island police will have the report of someone nearly abducting her while on the manta ray snorkel excursion. Call the cruise ship too. Tell them to talk to a steward named Sal Chopra. He knows the steward who delivered the flowers with the stalker's note. We have to find out who is behind this."

He knew he was raving and not making much sense. "Look, the police know all the backstory."

"Stay on the line, please."

"I can't. I have to find her! Look, you know where I am. Send help, please. She's everything to me. We have to find her!" His voice broke, and he ended the call before she could protest.

Shauna would have answered him if she was able. She'd either been abducted by someone or she'd been swept downstream and out to sea. He tried to think through everything they knew, but nothing seemed obvious. He needed some support. He called up Otis's phone, but he only got his voice mail. He left a message asking his friend to call him back.

Two other tents were in the area. With nothing to lose and no other ideas to try, he went to each one and roused the occupants—a young couple in the green tent and two young men in the orange one. They all quickly joined him in the search when they heard what had happened.

"We'll walk down the stream and keep calling her name," one of the young college students said. "I didn't hear anything though."

The young woman in the green tent nodded. "Me neither."

"Did you see anyone skulking around acting suspicious earlier in the day?"

She frowned and pushed her tousled blonde hair out of her face. "There was this guy here earlier, an older dude. He crossed the stream to the other side, then returned and sat back in the trees looking around. I offered him a hot dog when we were grilling them, but he just glared at me with mean eyes."

"I don't suppose he told you his name?"

The young woman shook her head. "He wasn't talking."

"Do you remember what he looked like?"

"Like an aging surfer. You know the type. Streaked blondish hair in one of those stylish cuts that looked good in the sixties. About six feet tall." She glanced at her boyfriend. "Funny colored eyes, right? Kind of brownish green."

"Thanks." Hazel eyes. Raul's face flashed through his mind, but that was crazy. He hadn't even hung out with them all that much. It was ridiculous to even suspect him, but Zach knew in an instant that he was the one. He had to be. But why?

"We'll look the other way," the girl said.

Zach went back to the water and squinted in the moonlight, trying to make out anything on the other side. Nothing. He stalked along the swollen stream shouting her name as he waited for the helicopter with the police to arrive. He prayed for Shauna with everything in him. *Please, God, keep her safe.*

Chapter 12

Shauna's head throbbed like a sore tooth. She opened her eyes to dim light and the sound of waves. Her cheek was down in the sand, and her back ached from the weird angle she'd fallen into with her waist twisted to the side. She pushed herself up and blinked.

She was in some kind of cave. Soft sand led up into the cave, but the booming sound of waves echoed off the rocks surrounding her. An inflatable raft with a motor had been pulled up beside her, and she saw a man's head on the other side of the raft. Sleeping or just waiting until she awakened?

Her hair hung in disarray around her face, and she tugged out the hair tie to bind it up again. Last night was such a jumble. She'd recognized the man, hadn't she? Right now she couldn't quite grasp that memory. Whatever he'd injected her with had left her head fuzzy.

The man's head turned at the snap of the hair tie, and he leaned forward. Her blood thundered in her ears, and she wished she had some kind of weapon, but there was nothing here but sand. That wouldn't go far. She held her breath and rose to her feet to face him.

She went faint as her memory flooded back. "Raul? What have you done?"

Raul stood and smiled. Why had she ever thought he was nice looking for a man his age? There was nothing handsome about the cruel tilt to his lips or the possessive gleam in his eyes. She backed away as he came around the boat toward her.

"Hungry?" He gestured to the boxes stacked in the back of the sea cave. "There's just about anything you could want."

"I'm not hungry. You haven't answered me." She kept her tone cold. "Why would you do this, Raul? I want to go back to my campsite. Right now."

"I'm afraid we can't go anywhere until you remember, Shannon."

She frowned and took another step back. "My name

is Shauna, not Shannon. Shannon was your wife. She's dead, Raul."

He blinked and flinched just a bit. "You'll remember who you really are soon enough, my dear. I knew the minute I saw you in Honolulu that you'd come back to me. You'd always said you'd find a way, and you did." He beamed at her as if she'd done something amazing.

"I'm Shauna. Shauna Bannister."

She had to figure out a way to get him to see reality. His delusions could get them both killed. How had he even gotten her here in these rough seas?

His smile remained fixed. "It will all come back to you, my darling. Not even death can separate us. You'll forget all about Bannister once you remember who you really are."

He walked to the boxes and rummaged inside. "Let's get some food in us. I even have a little propane stove to heat up our soup."

Did he really think she was going to praise him for thinking ahead? She wouldn't take anything from him if she was starving—and her stomach rebelled at the very thought of food. She needed to get out of here.

She darted to the boat and started to drag it to the water, but he was at her side in moments. He pushed her aside and secured the boat again. The stare he turned on her made her shiver.

"Please, Raul. You have to get me back to Zach. He'll be going out of his mind with worry. And I have a little boy, Alex, remember? He needs his mommy. You wouldn't want to be the one responsible for leaving him motherless."

Something flickered in his eyes, but before she could decide whether it was regret or awareness, he swung back to the food. He prepared peanut butter sandwiches. He put one on a paper plate and handed it to her. "Eat. We'll get through this, Shannon. You just have to listen to me."

He squinted toward the lowering clouds in the opening to the sea cave. "I hadn't wanted to leave here until you remembered, but if we get a storm, this little bit of beach will be gone. I need to think of where else we can go to be alone." He prodded her arm with a hard hand. "If you don't eat, I'll hold your head underwater until you do. Sometimes punishment is the only thing that works."

The thread of madness in his words encouraged her to force down a tasteless bite of the sandwich. How could she get through to him? He was truly insane.

Wait a minute—what if she played up that angle and pretended to remember? If she could convince him she thought he was right, maybe he'd get them back to a town where she could scream for help.

She had to think this through though and try to remember what she'd heard about Shannon, little though it was. She'd died of cancer, and they would have been married thirty-five years. She was afraid of water too. That was about the sum of Shauna's knowledge of the woman. If only she had her phone so she could look up a few things.

If he thought she was playing him, he would likely use that "punishment" he'd threatened.

❧

By the time the sun was fully up, Zach could only pace back and forth as the police officers talked. The police detective, a Hawaiian in his forties, approached him. Kaeo Iona was a big man with an alert manner and shrewd dark eyes. He wore his long black hair tied at the back of his neck. Zach had immediately trusted him.

"Well, Zach, we've turned up some interesting things in the past hour. Your acquaintance Raul Jackman rented an inflatable raft with a motor. According to his Facebook page, he's an avid boater. We've questioned the steward you mentioned, and one of his friends delivered the flowers to your room. Mr. Jackman paid him a hundred dollars to take them to the suite."

Zach had known it in his bones. "But why? He only met Shauna a week ago."

"He was staying at the same hotel as you were in Honolulu. All I can assume is that he saw her and became obsessed." He turned his phone around to show Zach. "Look here. I found a copy of his wedding picture. The woman look familiar?"

Zach barely bit back a gasp. "Shannon looks a lot like Shauna with the black hair and green eyes. The shape of the face is different and Shannon's taller, but I could see why he'd be drawn to her."

"I don't know your wife, but I saw her picture, and I thought the same thing. So maybe this old dude wants her to replace his wife?"

"I guess it's possible. The question is how do we find her?"

"Well, we know he has an inflatable. He must have hired someone to bring the boat to the beach in case he could grab her. I had some officers cross the stream with the rope. They're experienced, but it's not something I'd recommend, by the way. They found drag marks at the beach where an inflatable was pulled to the water."

"He couldn't have known she would cross the stream and be trapped though. It doesn't make sense."

"I suspect he planned to grab her at an opportune time. If she hadn't left the tent on her own, he might have killed you and taken her. I have all the ports on high alert, but with an inflatable, he could pull in at just about any of the beaches. Many of them aren't manned by lifeguards. I know one thing though—he can't get off the island with her. Airport security is on the lookout, and they'll be spotted."

Zach voiced one of his biggest fears. "What if he plans to kill her? Maybe he wants to die with her or something."

Iona's dark eyes went more somber. "Definitely something we have to keep in mind. We need to find them. I've alerted the Coast Guard, and they're patrolling the waters looking for an inflatable. Try to stay calm. I think we'll find them. He has to be trying to get back to town."

Zach balled up his fists. Thinking it and knowing it were two different things. "Thanks, Detective." He walked away and went to stand at the water's edge. The Na Pali coastline was intimidating as it loomed up out of the valley.

He walked back to Iona. "Detective, what's along the Na Pali coastline? Any other towns?"

Iona shook his head. "Rocks, a few small beaches, sea caves. No towns or anything. It's not accessible by land at all, and even by air you'd be hard-pressed to land a chopper."

"He has that inflatable. We could check the beaches and the sea caves."

"A small boat can navigate it, but the seas are rough this time of year. Big swells traveling all the way from Australia. The excursion companies don't take small boats out after September."

"But he's crazy enough to try it. You said he was an avid boater. Maybe he thinks he can handle it."

Iona pressed his lips together and fell silent for a moment. "Well, we could check it."

"How many with areas to land?"

"Maybe not so many," he admitted. "Okay, I'll put a call into the Coast Guard and tell them we want to check that direction too."

"I'd like to come along."

Iona started to shake his head, then stopped and looked at Zach. "If I say no, you'll just go rent a boat, won't you?"

"Yep. She's my wife and I have to find her." His voice wobbled a bit, and he cleared his throat. "I'm former Coast Guard. I know my way around a boat."

"Okay. Don't get in the way."

"Thank you, Detective."

Iona gave a grunt and turned toward the helicopter. "Get in."

Chapter 13

Shauna sat in the rear of the sea cave with her back against the rocks. Raul was making preparations to leave the cave, but the swells crashing into the rocks terrified her. She couldn't imagine being out there in the middle of those seas with only the protection of the flimsy inflatable. Though it had a motor, she doubted it would be able to navigate those mountainous waves.

"I don't want to go out there, Raul. You know how water scares me."

He dropped another box of supplies into the boat, then turned a smile on her. "You're starting to remember, Shannon, aren't you? Shauna claimed not to be afraid of water."

She forced a smile. "I-I'm not sure where that fear is coming from. How can I be Shannon?"

His gaze intent, he squatted in front of her. "Do you remember when we went to India in 1985? We visited quite a few Hindu temples, and we were both enthralled with their beliefs. You told me if anything happened to either of us, we had to promise we'd come back and find each other. Standing on the banks of the Ganges, your eyes were so intent, so beautiful, as you made your promise.

"Deep down I didn't really believe it, but after cancer took you, I began to watch for your reincarnated soul. I never found you and had begun to give up hope. That is, until I spotted you at the hotel in Honolulu. Do you remember being reborn, Shannon? When is Shauna's birthday?"

Shauna didn't want to answer because it would feed into his obsession, but maybe she could use it to her advantage. "April 14, 1986."

"What time?"

"Nine at night."

The lines on his face smoothed out, and his eyes glittered. "Shannon died April 14 at fifteen minutes until nine. I think that proves it."

Shauna barely suppressed a shudder. There were

many Bible verses she could have quoted to refute his belief, but she needed to convince him she was buying into his theory. She had a strong sense of self, of who she was in the Lord. Otherwise, his passion and delusion might have confused her.

"T-That's pretty persuasive." She looked away so he couldn't read her expression. She might not be able to hold back her disdain and disbelief.

"I knew you'd see it. Wait until you see the home I've built for you, Shannon. Hindu shrines and beautiful Hindu architecture. There's a temple on the grounds. I'm sorry now that I had begun to doubt. I'd even thought of selling it because I was beginning to despair of ever seeing you again."

A shiver ran down her back. She prayed for God to lead Zach in the right search. This man terrified her.

She'd been keeping an eye on the weather, and she didn't see any way to avoid going out in those swells. The minuscule sliver of beach was rapidly disappearing. "Can we go there now? I-I really want to see it."

His fingers gripped her chin, and he raised her face until she met his gaze. She pretended it was Zach across from her and put as much love into her expression as she could manage.

He blinked and smiled, then released her and stood. "Yes, let's go there now. I've got a small jet rented to take us back to California. We won't even have to deal with TSA or anything like that. I can pull my car right up to the plane, and we can board."

Her chest tightened. She'd counted on being able to ask for help. Maybe she could plead with the pilot for assistance. Once she was out of this sea cave, there would be other people around. There had to be.

He dragged the raft into the water as another huge swell washed over Shauna's feet and wet her legs up to the calves. "Hop in, honey. Let's get out of here."

The rubber was wet and slippery, and she half fell into the bottom of the boat, then crawled to the seat in the bow. She wanted to be able to see what was coming. Maybe she would find the opportunity to leap over-board and swim to a beach, though in these seas, that hope seemed remote.

Raul waded into the waves and dragged the raft the rest of the way off the last strip of beach. The engine roared to life with one tug, and he steered the boat for the exit. Out of the shelter of the sea cave, the swells seemed even taller, and the sky spit rain in short bursts.

The clouds blotted out the sun, and the wind whipped Shauna's ponytail all around.

She had no real idea where they were, other than the Na Pali coastline. Polihale should be to the south of this spot, and when he turned in that direction, she breathed a sigh of relief. Civilization was that way. Maybe the Coast Guard was looking for her by now too.

The craft rode up the swells, then down the slope in a drop that made her stomach plunge. She prayed constantly for rescue and safety as Raul, his face grim and set, fought with the boat. Was he worried at all? Maybe obsession didn't allow any doubts.

The sea spray drenched her in just a few minutes, and she licked the salt from her lips. Her eyes burned from the salt as well. The violent heaving of the boat threatened to toss her into the water at any minute, and her fingers hurt from gripping the side of the raft. She scanned the horizon with the desperate hope of seeing a big Coast Guard cutter heading their way.

Raul hadn't said anything since they clashed with the waves, and she spared him a quick look. He was grinning with wild exultation as if he reveled in the battle with the sea. Maybe he did. Madness like his was hard to understand, and she didn't really care to figure him out. All she wanted to do was escape.

✧

Shauna's fingers had gone numb from holding on to the raft, and every muscle in her arms and back throbbed with exertion. Just when she thought the swells couldn't get any taller, they grew even more mountainous. Hadn't they been fighting the waves in front of this particular stretch of coastline for an hour? They seemed to be making little headway against the wind.

The rain came down in earnest now. Her teeth chattered, and she huddled on the floor to try to avoid the wind as much as possible.

Swathed in the only life jacket, Raul muttered to himself as he stared out at the wind and waves. His earlier determination and struggle with steering the boat had ebbed, and he sat with his hand slack on the motor as if uncaring what was going to happen. Shauna knew a little about boats and motors but not enough to battle what they were facing.

Raul said something, and following his line of sight, she peeked her head above the rim of the raft to see the biggest swell yet barreling down on them. Then it struck the boat, and she was airborne. Her feet and arms pinwheeled before she came crashing down into the sea.

The waves closed over her head and tossed her like flotsam in a flood until she didn't know which way the air was that her lungs burned for. She saw a faint light and kicked toward it. Her head broke the surface, and she looked around for the boat. It floated upside down twenty feet away, and she tried to swim toward it, but the waves claimed her again and pushed her in the opposite direction. She saw no sign of Raul.

Her arm throbbed, and she saw a small, bleeding abrasion on her right forearm. She must have scraped it on the motor or a box when she was flung into the sea. Would the blood attract sharks? She pushed away the fear that would serve no purpose right now. There was nothing she could do to fix it.

The Na Pali coastline was to her left, only about a hundred feet, but she saw no place to pull herself ashore without being dashed against the razor-sharp rocks. Fighting to keep her head above the waves quickly sapped her strength, and she gulped in seawater. She looked around again for the raft, but it was much farther away, too far to reach in these swells.

She was going to drown. The thought didn't bring fear, just the sting of regret that she'd be leaving Alex motherless. She'd be leaving Zach when she'd just found him.

A splash sounded behind her, and she saw Raul thrashing in the water. His lips were blue, but his eyes were clear. His life vest was in his hands, and he threw it at Shauna.

"Put it on," he rasped. "I'm a strong swimmer. I can make it. Follow me, Shannon. I'll help you. I can't lose you when I've just found you."

She wasn't going to argue with him and had on the life vest in another minute. While the waves still pummeled her, it was easier to keep her head above water with the help of the flotation device.

She looked around and saw Raul striking out with strong strokes for the coastline. Did he see something she didn't? She started to follow him, but she wasn't strong enough to fight the current and decided to let it carry her farther south. The problem was it was also dragging her away from the shore.

She couldn't worry about that now. All she could do was pray and try to stay alive as long as she could. For Alex. For Zach. She didn't want to die before she saw Connor and Brenna again either.

Her eyelids were so heavy. She kept closing them and drifting in a happy place where Zach carried her in his strong arms along the beach in the warm sun.

A cold wave washed over her face and brought her fully awake. She blinked the sting of salt out of her eyes. Where was the shore? She was alone in a vast sea with no idea in which direction she should swim.

No, not alone. God was out here with her. Whatever happened, she was safe in his arms.

Chapter 14

The Coast Guard cutter rode the waves hard, often smashing down into the seas like the roughest log ride imaginable. His legs braced against the wind and the rocking ride, Zach stood in the bow with a pair of binoculars and scanned the big rollers for a glimpse of Shauna's face in the water. They'd seen nothing yet, but he had to hang on to his hope.

This storm had swept in so suddenly, and he'd overheard a couple of the Coasties say they hoped Shauna and Raul weren't trying to shelter in a sea cave. These swells would make that impossible. Would Raul have figured that out? Surely he'd paid attention to the forecasts.

Iona, clad in a waterproof Windbreaker, came to join him. "Anything?"

Not trusting himself to speak, Zach shook his head. Iona held out his hand to a Coastie with another set of binoculars. "May I?" The detective adjusted the eyepiece and swept them back and forth in a practiced motion.

Zach went back to searching as well. He'd done this many times when he was in the Coast Guard, but he never thought he'd be searching open seas for his wife. "Wait a second."

"What is it?" Iona asked.

"Might be a boat. Hard to tell." Zach told him where to look.

"You're right." Iona went to direct the boat navigator.

Zach adjusted the binoculars again and scanned the waves. A glimpse of green caught his eye. Could that be a boat? If it was, it rode low in the water. Maybe capsized.

The cutter sped up and headed in the direction of whatever was in the water. Zach held on to the rail. "Please, Lord, let us find her alive." His lips felt numb as he prayed the same plea over and over again.

As the boat neared the site, his gut tightened. It was an inflatable boat, mostly submerged. There was no sign of Shauna or Raul. The motor slowed on the Coast Guard cutter, and a diver leaped into the water to investigate. Zach kicked off his shoes and went in after him. Shauna could be under there.

A big swell lifted him up and deposited him closer to the capsized inflatable. He dove under the boat and looked around to make sure Shauna wasn't trapped. Nothing there but a floating jar of peanut butter. He swam out from under the inflatable and searched the waves.

Iona and some of the Coast Guard guys were motioning for them to return. They must have seen something. He swam quickly back to the boat and climbed the ladder behind the diver.

He was gasping for breath when he stepped on deck. "What's happened?"

Iona pointed. "There's someone swimming close to the rocks there. From this distance we can't tell whether it's a man or a woman, but they're alive."

It had to be Shauna. Zach ran to his spot at the front of the ship and held on to the railing as the bow lifted out of the water and practically flew across the top of the waves toward the floundering swimmer. Zach grabbed the binoculars and trained them on the figure struggling against the waves. His hope crashed.

"It's Raul," he told Iona.

"That means Shauna should be around here somewhere."

The boat slowed as it neared Shauna's stalker, and two swimmers went overboard to help haul him to safety. In minutes Raul was gasping on the deck. The man was blue and trembling. He saw Zach and turned his face away.

Zach wanted to grab him and shake him, but he clenched his fists and knelt by his side. "Where is she?"

"Shannon's fine. She's fine. I made sure of it. I gave her my life vest."

"Her name is Shauna. Where is she?" he growled.

"The last I saw of her she was drifting out to sea. But she'll be fine. I gave her a life vest. I couldn't lose her when she'd just come back to me. My beloved Shannon."

Zach couldn't listen to the man's raving anymore. Not without wanting to choke the life out of him. He rose and went to grab the binoculars again. She had to be out there somewhere, waiting for him to find her.

Hang on, Fly Girl. I'm coming.

So tired. The cold and fatigue slowed her mind and muscles. Shauna floated on her back as much as possible and stared up at the sky. A bit of blue was beginning to peek through the glowering clouds. The glimpse of the sun was like a tiny ray of hope in a gray world.

Hold on, Fly Girl.

Her eyes flew open, and she searched for Zach. She could imagine him saying those words as he searched frantically for her. She knew he was out there some-where, doing his best to find her. She had to do her part too. Knowing Zach, he would mobilize the Navy if he had to, plus commandeer all of the Coast Guard boats stationed here.

She smiled at the thought. Her husband was single-minded in his devotion. She kicked her legs and looked around. If only she knew which way to swim. But wait, the clouds had parted enough that she could see the sun now. By this time it had to be afternoon, so the sun would be toward the west. She had to swim east, back toward the island. But was that right? She was too tired to work it out, but she had to try. Keeping the bit of sun to her back, she began to put some effort into swim-ming. *Stroke, kick, stroke, kick.*

If nothing else, the effort lifted her mood and made

her believe she could survive this, that she would see Alex and Zach again. That she would hold Connor and Brenna in her arms after all these years.

Something gleamed in the water in the dim light. Was that a shark? *No, God, please, no!*

Her lungs squeezed, and she tried to stop kicking so she didn't attract its attention, but a big wave crashed over her head, and she went under. She had to try or she'd drown. Kicking her legs, she surfaced and coughed the sting of saltwater out of her lungs.

Where was it? The terror nearly overwhelmed her when she saw the fin even closer. Would death come quickly, or would she feel every bit of the pain from being eaten? She gasped and inhaled water. *Breathe, breathe.*

Wait, there was more than one fin. Dolphins. It was a dolphin pod. Tears stung her eyes. *Thank God, thank God.*

She gradually became aware of a throbbing noise in the air, and she looked up to see if there was a chopper coming her way, but no. The sky held only disappearing clouds as the storm began to pass.

Maybe it was her blood thundering in her ears from fatigue and exertion. With the sun at her back, she began to swim again. Where was the land? Was she even making any headway against the current?

The sound grew louder, and she paused again to turn around in the water. Then she saw it. A boat! Was there a more beautiful sight than that white bow cutting through the blue waves?

She waved her hands. "Here! I'm here!"

The boat didn't slow but continued to move past her. Didn't anyone on board see her? She shouted again, "I'm here!"

She heard a responding shout, then the boat slowed. Someone jumped into the water, and she swam in that direction. In moments she saw his beloved face. Zach. He'd come for her, just as she'd known he would. Her vision blurred as he reached her and pulled her close.

"I've got you, Fly Girl."

A sob escaped and she clung to her husband. She'd tried to be so strong, but it was over. Raul hadn't been able to defeat them.

A flotation device landed near them, and Zach grabbed it, thrusting his arm through the center hole. "Hang on to me, honey. They'll pull us in."

"I don't ever want to let you go." She wrapped both arms around his waist and pressed her cheek against his wet chest.

They reached the side of the boat, and eager hands

reached down to lift them both up. Someone draped a warm blanket around her, and someone else thrust a hot cup of coffee into her hands. It was a little slice of heaven.

But mostly, all she wanted to do was stay in the circle of Zach's embrace and thank God that he'd saved her, saved them both from Raul's terrible plans.

She nestled against Zach as they huddled together in the blanket. "I was so scared I'd never see you again, Zach. That I'd never see Alex or Connor or Brenna. But you came."

His grip on her tightened. "Always, Shauna. Always. I asked God to hold you up until I found you."

"And he did."

Zach pressed a warm kiss on her cold lips, and the passion in him heated her blood, chasing away the last of the shivers. "I knew he would."

"How'd you know I was out there?"

"We hauled Raul out of the water. He said you were drifting out to sea, so we headed out to look. It's a miracle we found you in these seas."

"He's under arrest now?"

"Yeah, he's down in the hold. Detective Iona will file a ton of charges against him. I doubt he'll get out of jail anytime soon."

"Did we miss the cruise ship leaving port?"

"Yeah, it left at two, but it's a short flight to Honolulu. We just have to be there by four tomorrow to catch our flight to North Carolina. I can reschedule that though. It's been quite an ordeal."

She turned her face against him and sighed. "I found out I was stronger than I thought. It was scary, but I had such peace out there, Zach—such faith that God would hold me no matter what happened. I don't ever want to forget it."

She could feel him nod against the top of her head and knew he'd felt it too. "Let's find a peaceful hotel to hole up in for the night. I want the biggest lobster we can find for dinner, and I want to watch the sunset with you one last time in paradise."

"Wherever you are is paradise for me," he murmured against her hair.

She smiled and rested against him. Safe. He made her feel safe and treasured. This was a honeymoon no one could ever forget, and she would try to hold on to every memory. Or maybe only the good ones.

She lifted her face to his. "Kiss me, Cowboy."

His kiss grounded her and promised a lifetime of passion, trust, and commitment. Everyone should be so lucky.

Discussion Questions

1. Where is your dream vacation? No matter how many times we go, mine will always be Hawaii.
2. Have you ever witnessed obsession? If so, how did you deal with it?
3. Has an experience ever caused you to have lingering fear that changes your behavior?
4. Have you ever faced death like Shauna? If you have, how did you cope?
5. Shauna turned to God during trying times. How do you cope with challenging circumstances?
6. Have you ever experienced what you knew was God's hand working in your life?
7. Most people are a mix of good and evil like Raul. Have you ever seen someone turn around and leave evil behind?

Acknowledgments

I'm so blessed to belong to the terrific HarperCollins Christian Publishing dream team. I've been with my great fiction team for fifteen years, and they are like family to me. I learn something new with every book, which makes writing so much fun for me!

Our fiction publisher and editor, Amanda Bostic, is as dear to me as a daughter. She really gets suspense and has been my friend from the moment I met her all those years ago. Fabulous cover guru Kristen Ingebretson works hard to create the perfect cover—and does. And, of course, I can't forget the other friends in my amazing fiction family: Becky Monds, Kristen Golden, Allison Carter, Jodi Hughes, Paul Fisher, Matt Bray, Kimberly Carlton, and

Kayleigh Hines. You are all such a big part of my life. I wish I could name all the great folks at HCCP who work on selling my books through different venues. I'm truly blessed!

Julee Schwarzburg is a dream editor to work with. She totally gets romantic suspense, and our partnership is pure joy. She brought some terrific ideas to the table with this book—as always!

My agent, Karen Solem, has helped shape my career in many ways, and that includes kicking an idea to the curb when necessary. We are about to celebrate fifteen years together! And my critique partner of twenty years, Denise Hunter, is the best sounding board ever. Thanks, friends!

I'm so grateful for my husband, Dave, who carts me around from city to city, washes towels, and chases down dinner without complaint. My kids—Dave, Kara (and now Donna and Mark)—love and support me in every way possible, and my little granddaughter, Alexa, makes every day a joy. She's talking like a grown-up now, and having her spend the night is more fun than I can tell you. Our little grandson, Elijah, is fourteen months old as I write this, and we look forward to his baby brother's arrival in May. Exciting times!

Most important, I give my thanks to God, who has opened such amazing doors for me and makes the journey a golden one.

The JOURNEY CONTINUES
back in LAVENDER TIDES!

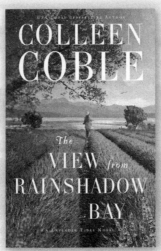

Available in print, e-book, and audio

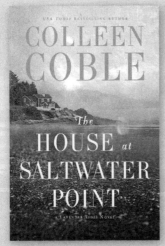

Available July 2018

Available January 2019

THE
SUNSET COVE
series

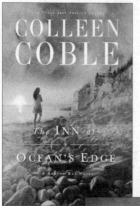

AVAILABLE IN PRINT,
E-BOOK, AND AUDIO

AVAILABLE IN PRINT,
E-BOOK, AND AUDIO

AVAILABLE IN PRINT,
E-BOOK, AND AUDIO

THE ROCK HARBOR *series*

Available in print, audio, and e-book

Read more from
COLLEEN COBLE!

About the Author

Colleen Coble is a *USA Today* bestselling author and RITA finalist best known for her romantic suspense novels, including *Tidewater Inn*, *Rosemary Cottage*, and the Mercy Falls, Lonestar, Rock Harbor, and Sunset Cove series.

❧

Visit her website at www.colleencoble.com.
Twitter: @colleencoble
Facebook: colleencoblebooks